The Lyran Legacy

The Starseed Chronicles Begin

Lyran Legacy: The Starseed Chronicles Begin

Dedication

To my daughter, Dominique, and my granddaughter, Carter,
your love and light continue to inspire me every day.

To my husband, Franklin, thank you for your unwavering
support and endless love. You are my rock.

To my brother, Coach Bell, and my nephew, Tre,
your love and support mean more to me than words can say.

To my Uncle David, who taught me to be a keeper of your
word.

To my mother, Evelyn, who has returned to the stars.
You were the heart of our family, holding us all together with
your love. Your spirit lives on in everything I do.

And to all the Starseeds living on Earth,
dedicated to helping humanity transition to a new world filled
with harmony, unity, and love. This journey is for you, and
together, we will create a better future.

With all my love and gratitude,
Audrey Bell-Kearney

Lyran Legacy: The Starseed Chronicles Begin

Table Of Content:

Lyran Legacy: The Starseed Chronicles Begin

Introduction to *The Starseed Chronicles*

In the vast cosmos, beyond the stars we gaze upon each night, there exists a network of enlightened beings who have long watched over Earth. These beings, known as Starseeds, originate from distant star systems, galaxies, and dimensions beyond our wildest imaginations. Their mission is not one of conquest or dominance, but of healing, enlightenment, and awakening. For centuries, they have lived among us in silence, waiting for the moment when humanity would be ready to rise above its chaos and embrace a higher way of living.

Now, in an age of unprecedented turmoil and transformation, that time has come.

The Earth we know is changing—physically, spiritually, and energetically. The old systems that once defined our world are beginning to crumble, making way for something new. This is not the end; it is the beginning of The New Earth. An Earth where humanity's consciousness is elevated, where love and unity take precedence over fear and division, and where every being lives in harmony with one another and the planet itself.

But this transformation cannot happen alone.　·

The Starseeds, long aware of Earth's potential, have returned in greater numbers to guide humanity through this transition. They are healers, warriors, teachers, and visionaries, each one awakened to their cosmic origins and to the powerful mission that lies ahead. Hidden among the everyday lives of people, the Starseeds are preparing for the monumental task of helping humanity ascend to its next evolutionary phase—a phase where the Earth becomes a beacon of light within the universe.

Lyran Legacy: The Starseed Chronicles Begin

In this series, you will journey alongside the Starseeds as they awaken to their purpose, gather their forces, and embark on a mission to save humanity from itself. With each book, you will witness the birth of The New Earth and the cosmic battles—both seen and unseen—that will shape the destiny of all who inhabit this planet.

This is a story of hope, transformation, and the eternal fight between light and dark. The Starseeds have come to show us that a new world is possible. But the question remains: Will humanity embrace their guidance, or will it remain trapped in the cycles of its past?

The fate of The New Earth hangs in the balance. The Starseeds are here to tip the scales.

Welcome to The Starseed Chronicles. The journey begins now.

Amongst The Stars

In *The Starseed Chronicles*, the Starseeds originate from various star systems across the cosmos, each bringing unique energies, abilities, and knowledge to Earth. These star systems represent ancient civilizations that have long evolved beyond the material and spiritual limitations of Earth, and they have sent their emissaries—Starseeds—to help guide humanity through its ascension. Here are the main star systems where the Starseeds come from:

1. **Pleiades**: A star cluster also known as the "Seven Sisters." Many Starseeds believe they come from the Pleiades and are here to help humanity by bringing love, peace, and healing.
2. **Sirius**: The brightest star in the night sky. Starseeds from Sirius are often thought to bring knowledge of technology, spirituality, and wisdom to Earth.
3. **Arcturus**: A star in the constellation Boötes. Arcturian Starseeds are believed to be advanced beings who focus on emotional healing, compassion, and deep spiritual understanding.
4. **Orion**: The constellation Orion is also a common origin point. Starseeds from Orion are often seen as analytical, logical, and concerned with understanding the balance between light and dark.
5. **Lyra**: A constellation thought to be the origin of the human race according to some beliefs. Lyran Starseeds are believed to be pioneering and adventurous, bringing ancient knowledge to Earth.
6. **Andromeda**: A galaxy near the Milky Way. Andromedan Starseeds are said to be freedom seekers who are here to spread love and create a better world.
7. **Vega**: A star in the Lyra constellation, believed by some to be a source of knowledge and creativity.

8. **Other Dimensions or Parallel Universes**: Some Starseeds believe they come from different dimensions or parallel universes, where they exist in higher states of consciousness or non-physical forms.

Starseeds often feel a deep connection to these places, though this belief is spiritual and metaphysical rather than based on scientific evidence.

Chapter 1: The Destruction Of Lyra

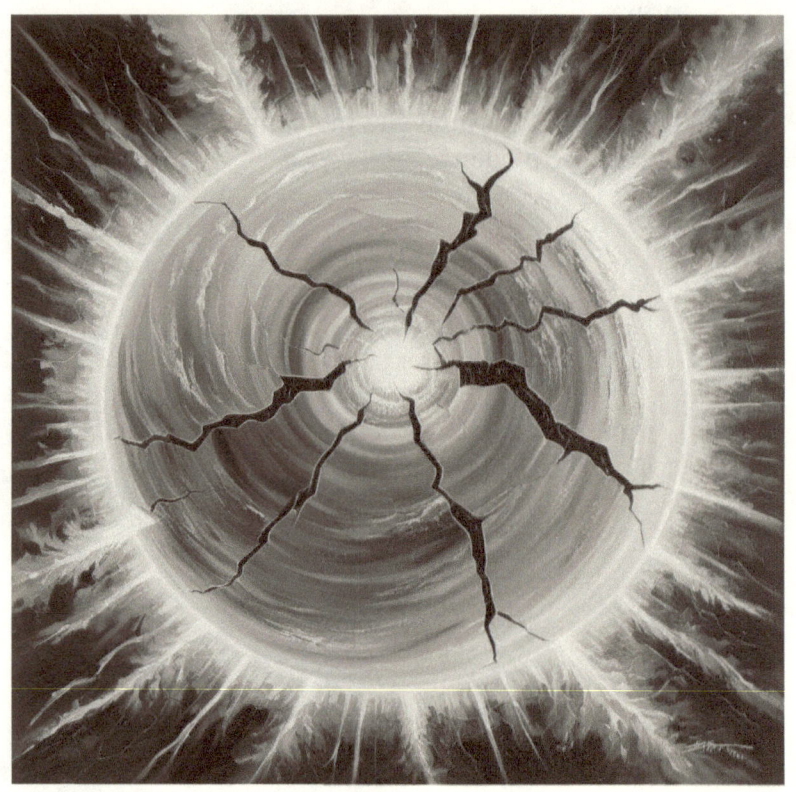

Lyran Legacy: The Starseed Chronicles Begin

In the vast expanse of the cosmos, where stars shimmer like distant jewels in the darkened sea of space, there was once a constellation unlike any other—Lyra. Among the countless worlds that orbited the stars, Lyra stood as a beacon of light, a place where harmony reigned and wisdom thrived. It was not merely a planet but a sanctuary, a cradle of enlightenment where the boundaries between the physical and the ethereal had long since blurred.

The Lyran people were the keepers of this world, a race of beings who had transcended the limitations of flesh and form. Their bodies, once solid like those of any other sentient race, had evolved over millennia. They were beings of light and energy, their forms radiant, shimmering in hues that reflected the crystalline beauty of their home. They were tall, elegant, and moved with a grace that seemed to mirror the celestial rhythms of the universe. The very essence of Lyra flowed through them, binding them to their world in a way that no other race in the galaxy could claim.

The twin suns that orbited Lyra bathed the planet in a perpetual glow—one that was neither too bright nor too dim. The light was perfect, a gentle golden hue that filled the skies with warmth and peace. Beneath those skies, the cities of Lyra glistened like fields of diamonds. Towers made of translucent crystal rose high into the heavens, their surfaces catching the light of the stars and refracting it in a kaleidoscope of colors. These cities were not built to dominate the landscape but to harmonize with it, as if they had grown organically from the earth itself, guided by the will of the Lyrans and their deep connection to their planet.

The natural world of Lyra was no less magnificent. Vast oceans, clear as glass, stretched across the horizon, their depths teeming with life forms as radiant and wondrous as the Lyrans themselves. Forests of towering trees, with leaves that shimmered in silvers and golds, covered the land, their branches swaying gently in a breeze that seemed to hum with the songs of the cosmos. It was said that these trees, known as **Sylvanis**, were older than time itself, having rooted themselves in the fabric of the universe when Lyra first came into being. The Lyrans believed that to walk among the Sylvanis was to walk with the stars, to hear the whispers of creation itself.

But it was not just the beauty of the landscape or the brilliance of their cities that made Lyra special. It was the profound spiritual connection the Lyrans shared with the universe. Unlike other civilizations that sought to conquer or manipulate the forces of nature, the Lyrans saw themselves as custodians. They were the guardians of cosmic knowledge, entrusted with the secrets of energy, time, and existence. Their civilization had long ago unlocked the mysteries of the stars, and with that knowledge, they had built a society free from suffering, strife, and conflict. They had no need for war, for they had transcended the petty desires that often led to destruction.

The Lyrans lived by the philosophy of **Unity**, a belief that all things were connected—every star, every planet, every being. To harm one was to harm all. It was this belief that had shaped their culture, their art, their music, and their way of life. To an outsider, Lyra would have seemed a paradise, a place untouched by the pain and struggle of other worlds. But for the Lyrans, it was simply home—a reflection of their inner selves, a mirror of the balance they had cultivated within.

Lyran Legacy: The Starseed Chronicles Begin

At the heart of their civilization stood the **Crystal Citadel**, a vast temple that housed the most powerful energy crystals in the galaxy. These crystals were not merely decorative; they were the lifeblood of Lyra, the source of the planet's harmony and the conduit through which the Lyrans communicated with the stars. Each crystal was attuned to the frequencies of the universe, allowing the Lyrans to tap into the cosmic energies that flowed through all things. It was through these crystals that they maintained their connection to the greater universe, ensuring that their actions always aligned with the balance of the cosmos.

But despite the peace and beauty that surrounded them, the Lyrans knew that the universe was not without its shadows. There were forces in the cosmos that did not share their reverence for life, forces that sought not to harmonize but to dominate. The Lyrans, in their wisdom, had always avoided these conflicts, choosing instead to retreat into the safety of their constellation, far from the violence that plagued other worlds. They believed that their isolation would protect them, that the purity of their existence would be enough to shield them from the darker currents of the universe.

Yet, as the stars shifted and the seasons of the cosmos turned, there were whispers—subtle at first, barely noticeable, but growing in intensity. The Elders of Lyra, the wise and ancient Council that guided the planet, began to sense it—a disturbance in the flow of energy, a tremor in the harmony that had always sustained them. It was as if the stars themselves were warning them of an approaching storm, one that threatened to shatter the peace they had so carefully cultivated.

The leader of the Council, **Elder Kallaris**, was the first to speak of these signs. He was a figure of great wisdom, his form more radiant than any other, and his voice carried the weight of the stars themselves. "The balance is shifting," he had said in one of the Council's gatherings. "I fear a darkness is rising, one that we may not be able to escape."

The other Elders listened, their forms glowing softly in the dim light of the Citadel. **Maestra Illana**, the Keeper of the Crystals, nodded slowly. She had felt the tremors as well, the subtle vibrations in the crystal energy fields that indicated a disturbance beyond their world. "The crystals hum with an unfamiliar resonance," she said. "Something is coming. But what it is, I cannot say."

Varaen, the youngest of the Elders and a brilliant philosopher, stood at the edge of the gathering, his mind racing with thoughts of what this could mean. He had always believed that Lyra's destiny was tied to the stars, that their existence had a purpose beyond their own world. But now, as the whispers of the cosmos grew louder, he wondered if that purpose was about to be tested in ways they had never imagined.

As the Council debated, the skies above Lyra remained calm, the twin suns casting their golden light over the world. Yet, beneath the surface of that calm, there was a tension, a sense of unease that even the youngest Lyrans could feel. It was as if the very air around them had changed, as if the planet itself was holding its breath, waiting for something to break the peace that had defined their existence for so long.

And so, the Lyrans waited, their eyes turned to the stars, their hearts filled with both hope and dread. They did not yet know the name of the darkness that approached, nor could they foresee the tragedy that would soon befall their world. But deep within their souls, they understood that the age of Lyra, the age of peace and harmony, was drawing to a close. A new chapter was about to begin—one that would reshape their destiny and send them on a journey far beyond the stars they had called home for so long.

The Elders of Lyra were not strangers to the rhythms of the universe. For countless generations, they had studied the stars and the delicate energies that flowed between them. They understood that existence itself was a fragile balance—one that required careful guardianship. It was this balance that had allowed their civilization to flourish while others crumbled under the weight of their own desires for power and control.

Lyra had always been a sanctuary, a beacon of light in the vastness of space. From the beginning of their history, the Lyrans had been devoted to preserving the harmony of their world. Their lives were intertwined with the pulse of the cosmos, and their knowledge of the universe extended far beyond their own constellation. They believed that every living thing, from the smallest creature to the brightest star, was part of an interconnected web of energy. To disturb one thread was to disturb the whole. It was this philosophy that guided them, shaping their actions and their relationship with the wider universe.

But now, for the first time in millennia, there was a disturbance in that web. The Elders had felt it—a shift, subtle yet undeniable, in the flow of energy that reached their planet. It was as if the stars themselves were trying to communicate, sending warnings through the cosmic currents that only the most attuned Lyrans could perceive.

Elder Kallaris, ever the watchful guardian, was the first to notice the change. He had spent countless nights meditating beneath the great spires of the Crystal Citadel, his consciousness expanding beyond the limits of his physical form, reaching out into the vastness of space. It was in these moments of deep connection that he had first felt the tremors—faint but unmistakable—rippling through the energy fields of the universe. At first, he had dismissed them as a natural fluctuation, a minor disturbance in the ebb and flow of cosmic forces. But as the days turned into weeks, the tremors grew stronger, more pronounced. Something was coming.

Kallaris had shared his concerns with the Council, but there had been hesitation. Lyra had known peace for so long, the idea of a true threat seemed almost inconceivable to some of the Elders. After all, the Lyrans had always remained apart from the wars and conflicts that had ravaged other worlds. They believed that their wisdom, their understanding of the universe, would protect them from such violence.

Maestra Illana, however, was not so sure. As the Keeper of the Crystals, she was intimately connected to the energies that sustained their world. The crystals, ancient and powerful, resonated with the vibrations of the stars. They were the lifeblood of Lyra, the source of its beauty, its strength, and its connection to the greater universe. It was through the crystals that the Lyrans had learned to harness the forces of nature, not to control them, but to work in harmony with them. And now, those very crystals were humming with a new and unfamiliar energy, one that seemed out of sync with the natural order.

"The crystals have never sung like this before," Illana had said during one of the Council's gatherings. Her voice, though calm, carried an edge of concern that had not gone unnoticed by the other Elders. "They pulse with a frequency I do not recognize. It is as if they are trying to warn us of something, though I cannot yet decipher what that warning might be."

The Council had listened in silence, the weight of Illana's words settling over them like a shroud. The Lyrans were a people who believed deeply in the wisdom of the cosmos, and they knew that the crystals, as conduits of that wisdom, never spoke without reason. If the crystals were warning them, it was not something to be taken lightly.

But what could it mean? The Lyrans had lived in harmony with the universe for so long. What force could possibly seek to disrupt that harmony now?

It was Varaen who first voiced what the others had only dared to think in the privacy of their own minds.

"The Dracos."

The word hung in the air like a shadow, casting a chill over the gathering. The Dracos were a name from the past, a race that had once sought to dominate the galaxy through fear and conquest. They were ancient, powerful, and ruthless, and their hunger for control knew no bounds. The Lyrans had heard stories of their brutality, though they had never encountered them directly. The Dracos operated in the far reaches of the galaxy, far from Lyra's peaceful constellation. Or so the Lyrans had always believed.

"Do you truly believe they have returned?" one of the Elders asked, their voice barely above a whisper.

Varaen nodded slowly. "I have studied the patterns in the stars. The disturbances we have felt—there is a pattern to them, a growing intensity that follows the path of an approaching force. The Dracos have been silent for centuries, but I fear they are on the move once again. And if they are, it is only a matter of time before they reach Lyra."

The Council fell silent. Even Elder Kallaris, who had always been the calm voice of reason, could not deny the truth in Varaen's words. The Dracos were the embodiment of chaos, the antithesis of everything the Lyrans stood for. Where the Lyrans sought harmony, the Dracos thrived on conflict. Where the Lyrans cherished life and beauty, the Dracos sought only power and domination.

The thought of the Dracos returning to the galaxy was terrifying enough. But the idea that they might be coming for Lyra, a world that had never known war, was almost too much to comprehend.

"What would they want with us?" Illana asked, her voice tinged with both fear and disbelief. "We have nothing that they could possibly desire. We are a peaceful people. We pose no threat to them."

"They desire power," Varaen replied. "And there is no greater power in the galaxy than the crystals of Lyra."

It was true. The crystals of Lyra, though beautiful and serene, held within them a vast store of energy—energy that, in the wrong hands, could be used for unimaginable destruction. The Dracos, with their insatiable hunger for control, would stop at nothing to possess such power. And if they could not have it, they would surely destroy it.

For the first time in centuries, the Lyrans found themselves facing a decision they had never thought they would have to make. To fight was against their very nature, but to do nothing could mean the end of everything they had built.

Elder Kallaris rose from his seat, his form glowing softly in the dim light of the chamber. "We must prepare," he said, his voice steady and calm, though the weight of his words was heavy. "The Dracos are coming. And we must be ready, not just to defend our world, but to protect the legacy of Lyra for future generations. We cannot let the light of our world be extinguished."

The other Elders nodded in agreement, though there was no joy in the decision. The path ahead was uncertain, and the stakes had never been higher. But one thing was clear: Lyra's age of peace was coming to an end, and a new chapter in their history was about to begin—one that would test the very core of their existence.

The decision to prepare for what was to come weighed heavily on the Council, for it marked a profound shift in the Lyrans' understanding of their place in the universe. Until now, they had been custodians of peace, guardians of harmony, never entangled in the violent struggles of other worlds. War was a distant concept to them, a relic of lesser civilizations that had not yet ascended to the spiritual heights they themselves had reached.

But the Dracos, with their cold, calculating thirst for power, were a force that could not be ignored. Even the Lyrans, with all their wisdom and advanced knowledge, understood that there were beings in the universe who cared nothing for balance or unity. The Dracos were the embodiment of that truth—a race that thrived on chaos and domination. If the Lyrans did not act, their world would become just another conquest in the Dracos' endless march through the stars.

For days, the Council debated their next steps. To fight, even in self-defense, went against everything they believed in. Yet to allow the Dracos to take Lyra, or worse, destroy it, would be an unforgivable betrayal of their duty to protect the universe's cosmic balance. The Lyrans, in their wisdom, knew that the power of the crystals in the wrong hands could bring untold destruction, not just to Lyra but to countless other worlds.

"We must find another way," Maestra Illana had said during one of the Council's final meetings on the matter. Her form flickered faintly as she spoke, the soft glow of her energy dimming as the weight of their discussions took its toll. "There must be a path that does not lead to violence, a way to safeguard the crystals without succumbing to the darkness ourselves."

The Council chambers, vast and serene, echoed with her words. Outside, the twin suns of Lyra cast their golden light through the translucent walls of the Citadel, filling the room with a soft, almost otherworldly glow. It was a place of beauty and reflection, designed to inspire clarity of thought. But even here, in the heart of their wisdom, the answer to this dilemma seemed elusive.

Elder Kallaris, ever the voice of reason, spoke next. "I understand your hesitation, Maestra, as we all do. But we must be realistic. The Dracos do not negotiate. They do not understand the language of peace. If we offer them the crystals, they will not be satisfied. They will take what they want, and they will leave our world in ruin."

His words hung heavy in the air, and for a moment, there was silence. The truth of his statement was undeniable, and yet, to acknowledge it felt like a betrayal of everything the Lyrans stood for. They had always believed in the power of unity, in the idea that all beings, no matter how different, could coexist in harmony. But now, faced with the Dracos, that belief was being tested in ways they had never imagined.

It was Varaen who finally broke the silence. "Perhaps," he said slowly, his voice thoughtful, "there is a way to meet the Dracos without becoming like them."

The other Elders turned to him, their glowing forms shifting slightly in the dim light. Varaen was the youngest of them, but his mind was sharp, his insights often piercing through the complexities that sometimes clouded the Council's judgment.

"We are not warriors," he continued, "but we are not powerless. The crystals themselves are a source of immense energy. Perhaps, instead of using them for violence, we can use them to protect—to create a barrier, a shield that will prevent the Dracos from reaching us. If we cannot fight them, we can at least make it impossible for them to take what they desire."

There was a murmur of agreement among the Council members. The idea was bold, yet it resonated with their deepest values. To fight with weapons was unthinkable, but to use the natural power of their world to defend themselves—that was something they could embrace.

"It would take time," Illana said, her voice contemplative. "The crystals would need to be aligned perfectly, and the energy fields would have to be maintained. But it is possible. If we could harness their full power, we might be able to create a shield that even the Dracos could not penetrate."

Elder Kallaris nodded, his glowing form becoming brighter as the weight of his earlier words lifted slightly. "Then it is decided. We will not fight, but we will not allow the Dracos to destroy what we have built. We will protect Lyra, not with violence, but with the energy of the cosmos itself."

The decision brought a sense of relief to the Council, though it was tempered by the knowledge that their plan was not without risk. The crystals were powerful, but they were also fragile. To channel so much energy through them could be dangerous. If the alignment was off by even the smallest fraction, the resulting explosion could be catastrophic—not just for the Dracos, but for Lyra as well.

Yet, they had no other choice. The Dracos were coming, and they would not stop until they had what they wanted.

As the preparations began, the atmosphere on Lyra shifted. The Lyrans, who had always lived their lives in peaceful reflection, now moved with a quiet urgency. The crystal engineers worked day and night, carefully aligning the great energy stones that would form the protective shield. The scholars and philosophers, who once spent their days contemplating the mysteries of the universe, now studied the ancient texts, searching for any wisdom that might aid them in their efforts.

And yet, even as they prepared, there was a sense of unease that permeated the air. The Dracos had not yet arrived, but their presence was already being felt. The skies above Lyra, once filled with the soft glow of their twin suns, now seemed darker, more oppressive. The stars, which had always brought comfort and guidance, seemed distant and cold. It was as if the universe itself was holding its breath, waiting for the inevitable clash that was to come.

The Lyran people, though committed to their path, could not help but feel a deep sense of sadness. They had always believed that their world was a reflection of the greater harmony of the cosmos, a place where peace and beauty could thrive without fear of destruction. But now, as the shadow of the Dracos loomed ever closer, they realized that no world, no matter how enlightened, was immune to the forces of darkness.

Still, they held on to hope. The crystals, with their ancient power, had protected them for millennia. Perhaps, just perhaps, they could protect them once more.

Elder Kallaris stood at the edge of the Crystal Citadel, gazing out over the horizon. The great spires of their cities shimmered in the fading light, and the oceans below reflected the colors of the sky in a dazzling display of beauty. It was a sight he had seen countless times before, but tonight, it felt different—more fragile, more fleeting.

"We are not without hope," he whispered to himself, though his heart was heavy. "But the time of peace is ending. Lyra's fate is now tied to the stars, and the path ahead is uncertain."

As the sun dipped below the horizon, casting the world into twilight, the first Draco ship appeared in the distance—a dark silhouette against the fading light. The invasion had begun.

The first Draco ship appeared as a distant, ominous shadow, a stark contrast to the soft, golden glow that Lyra had always known. Its angular design and dark metallic surface reflected none of the light from the twin suns; it seemed to absorb it instead, casting a palpable sense of dread over the once-peaceful skies. As it drew nearer, the scale of the ship became clear—it was massive, a harbinger of the dark power that the Dracos wielded.

From the vantage point of the **Crystal Citadel**, Elder Kallaris watched in silence, his mind racing with thoughts of what was to come. Around him, the other Elders and scholars stood, their glowing forms dimmer than usual, reflecting the growing unease that had settled over the planet. The Lyrans had long believed in the power of balance, in the strength of unity with the universe. But as the Draco ship broke through the atmosphere, that faith was being tested in ways they had never imagined.

"The time has come," Varaen said quietly, stepping forward to stand beside Kallaris. His expression was resolute, though his eyes betrayed the weight of the moment. "The Dracos are here."

Kallaris nodded, his gaze never leaving the approaching ship. "We knew this day would come," he replied. "We have done all we can to prepare. Now we must trust in the power of the crystals."

But even as he spoke, doubt gnawed at the edges of his mind. The crystals were powerful, yes—but were they enough? The Lyrans had always relied on the harmony of the universe to guide and protect them, but the Dracos were not a force of nature. They were something else entirely— an aberration, a twisted reflection of the universe's potential for chaos and destruction. They did not follow the natural order; they sought to bend it to their will.

And now they had come for Lyra.

As the Draco ship descended, it was joined by others, each one identical in its terrifying design. The sky, once filled with the light of the twin suns, was now darkened by the shadow of the Draco fleet. From the ground, the Lyran cities, with their towering crystal spires and shimmering structures, stood in stark contrast to the cold, alien ships that hovered above them. It was a visual reminder of the fundamental difference between the two civilizations—one dedicated to peace, beauty, and balance, the other to conquest and domination.

In the heart of the **Crystal Citadel**, Maestra Illana worked tirelessly, overseeing the final preparations for the activation of the planetary shield. The crystals, carefully aligned and calibrated over the past weeks, hummed with a low, resonant frequency, their energy fields vibrating in perfect harmony. The air around them was thick with the power they generated, a tangible reminder of the immense force that lay within.

But Illana knew that harnessing such power came with great risk. The crystals, while a source of strength, were also delicate. If the energy fields became unstable, the resulting backlash could devastate Lyra as surely as any Draco weapon. It was a precarious balance, one that required absolute precision to maintain.

"We are nearly ready," Illana said, her voice calm but tinged with urgency. She turned to the group of crystal engineers who had been working alongside her. "Begin the final sequence. We must activate the shield before the Dracos land."

The engineers, their hands glowing softly as they manipulated the energy currents flowing through the crystals, moved with practiced precision. Each motion was deliberate, every adjustment made with the utmost care. They knew that the fate of their world rested on their success.

As the shield activation process began, a soft, pulsing light emanated from the crystals, spreading outward in concentric waves. The energy fields expanded, forming an invisible barrier around the planet, one that would, if all went as planned, protect Lyra from the Draco onslaught.

Outside, the Draco ships continued their slow descent, their dark forms looming larger with each passing moment. From the ground, the Lyran people watched in a mixture of awe and terror. They had never known war, never seen the face of true aggression. The sight of the Draco fleet filling the skies was something out of their darkest nightmares.

Within the Council chambers, the Elders gathered around Kallaris, their forms glowing softly in the dim light.

Though their faces were calm, the tension in the room was palpable. They had made their decision—to protect their world with the power of the crystals—but now, as the Dracos drew closer, the weight of that decision pressed down on them like never before.

"We must hold to our course," Kallaris said, his voice steady despite the growing tension. "The shield will protect us. We have trusted the crystals for millennia—they will not fail us now."

But even as he spoke, a sense of foreboding lingered in the air. The Dracos were unlike any enemy the Lyrans had ever faced. They did not fight with honor or respect for the natural balance of the universe. They fought with brutality, with overwhelming force, and with a singular goal—to dominate, to take what they wanted by any means necessary.

As the first of the Draco ships hovered just above the surface of the planet, a deep, resonant sound echoed through the atmosphere—a low, rumbling vibration that seemed to shake the very core of Lyra. The Lyrans, sensitive to the energy of the universe, felt it in their bones, a disruption in the natural order that sent ripples of unease through the population.

And then, without warning, the Dracos made their first move.

A beam of dark energy shot from the lead ship, striking the surface of the planet with a force that shook the ground beneath the Lyran cities. The crystal spires, usually so resilient, trembled under the impact, their surfaces vibrating with the force of the attack. It was a warning shot—a declaration of intent. The Dracos were here, and they would not be denied.

Inside the Crystal Citadel, the shield flared to life, its invisible energy field shimmering briefly as it absorbed the impact of the Draco assault. For a moment, there was silence, as if the planet itself was holding its breath, waiting to see what would happen next.

"The shield is holding," Illana reported, her voice calm but filled with a quiet tension. "But we cannot afford to underestimate the Dracos. They will test our defenses, and if they find a weakness, they will exploit it."

Kallaris nodded, his face set in grim determination. "Then we must ensure that they find no weakness. We will hold the shield as long as we can."

But even as he spoke, he knew that this was only the beginning. The Dracos were relentless, and their desire for the power of the crystals would drive them to keep attacking until either Lyra fell or they were forced to retreat. And as powerful as the Lyran shield was, it could only hold for so long.

Outside, the Draco ships continued their assault, beams of dark energy striking the shield again and again, each impact reverberating through the atmosphere. The ground beneath the Lyran cities shook with the force of the attacks, and the once-serene planet was now filled with the sound of battle—a sound that the Lyrans had never thought they would hear on their peaceful world.

The Dracos were coming, and the Lyrans were about to face their greatest test. As the skies darkened and the shield shimmered with each blow, the fate of Lyra hung in the balance.

The relentless barrage of energy from the Draco ships continued, each blast resonating through the shield with a deep, thunderous pulse that echoed across the entire planet. Beneath the surface, the Lyran cities, once bastions of peace and beauty, now seemed fragile, their crystalline structures trembling under the strain. The once-clear skies were now filled with streaks of dark energy, slicing through the atmosphere like cruel reminders of the impending destruction.

Inside the **Crystal Citadel**, the tension had reached a breaking point. The Lyran people, who had lived for millennia without fear or conflict, now faced the terrifying reality of what the Dracos were capable of. Their harmonious existence, their deep connection to the cosmos, was being tested in ways they had never prepared for. And yet, despite the overwhelming force bearing down on them, the Lyrans held on to hope.

Illana, standing at the center of the chamber, her form glowing with the soft light of the crystals, continued to oversee the shield's energy levels. The crystals pulsed in time with the attacks, their luminous bodies absorbing the impacts and converting them into energy that was funneled back into the protective barrier. But with each strike, the strain on the crystals became more apparent. The harmonious hum that had always accompanied their energy now wavered, a faint dissonance creeping into the sound.

"It's holding, but not for much longer," Illana said, her voice quiet but firm. She turned to Kallaris, who stood at her side, his expression grim. "The crystals weren't designed for this kind of sustained assault. They were meant to channel the natural energies of the universe, not withstand the brutality of war."

Kallaris nodded, his glowing eyes fixed on the display before him. "We knew this day would come. But you are right, Maestra. The crystals are powerful, but they are not indestructible. If we push them too far..."

His voice trailed off, the unspoken possibility hanging in the air between them. If the crystals failed, the shield would collapse, and Lyra would be left defenseless against the Dracos. The devastation would be unimaginable.

Varaen, who had been watching the proceedings in silence, stepped forward. "There may be another way," he said, his voice steady but carrying a sense of urgency. "We've been using the crystals to fuel the shield, but perhaps we can use them in a different way. Instead of maintaining the barrier, what if we focused all of their energy into one final, powerful burst? Something that could disrupt the Dracos' fleet—at least long enough for us to find another solution."

Illana turned to him, her brow furrowed. "You're suggesting we release the energy all at once? That could be incredibly dangerous. The crystals might not be able to handle the sudden surge. If they shatter, the consequences would be catastrophic—for us as well as the Dracos."

"I know the risks," Varaen replied. "But if we continue like this, the shield will fail. We need to do something, or the Dracos will destroy everything."

Kallaris considered the proposal, his mind racing through the possibilities. Varaen was right—if they did nothing, the outcome was certain. The shield would eventually collapse, and Lyra would fall. But to release the full power of the crystals in a single burst could also mean the destruction of the very world they were trying to save.

"How much time would it buy us?" Kallaris asked, his voice calm but tinged with the weight of the decision that lay before him.

"A surge of that magnitude would likely disable their ships temporarily, maybe long enough to force them to retreat," Varaen said. "But it's impossible to predict exactly how long the disruption would last. It could be minutes, it could be hours. We'd need to use that time to evacuate the most important elements of our civilization—our people, our knowledge. We can't save Lyra, but we can save what matters most."

The words hit Kallaris like a blow to the chest. The idea of abandoning Lyra, of leaving behind the world they had nurtured for so long, was almost too much to bear. But the survival of their people, of their legacy, was more important than any single world. Lyra had been their home, but it was not their only hope.

He turned to Illana, whose eyes were filled with both fear and understanding. She nodded, though her expression remained solemn. "It's risky, but I believe we can do it. If we can control the release, we may be able to direct the energy outward, away from the surface, minimizing the damage to our own world."

Kallaris took a deep breath, the weight of the moment pressing down on him. This decision would define the future of their civilization, perhaps even the future of the galaxy. But there was no turning back now.

"Very well," he said, his voice filled with resolve. "Begin the preparations. We will release the energy and hope that it buys us the time we need."

The Council moved swiftly, their glowing forms moving through the chamber as they issued commands and coordinated the efforts of the crystal engineers. Every Lyran on the planet seemed to understand, instinctively, that this was their final stand. As the preparations were made, the once-quiet atmosphere of Lyra buzzed with a kind of frenetic energy, as if the planet itself was bracing for what was to come.

In the skies above, the Dracos continued their relentless assault, their dark beams of energy pounding against the shield with increasing intensity. But the Lyrans did not falter. They worked quickly, efficiently, their minds focused on the task at hand.

Finally, after what felt like an eternity, the moment arrived.

The crystals, aligned perfectly in the chamber, hummed with a deep, resonant energy that filled the air around them. Illana stood at the center of the array, her hands glowing as she manipulated the energy flows, guiding them into a single, powerful stream.

"It's ready," she said, her voice barely a whisper as the intensity of the energy built to a crescendo. "On your command, Elder Kallaris."

Kallaris stepped forward, his eyes locked on the crystals, their radiant forms pulsing with the full power of Lyra's ancient energy. This was it—the moment that would determine the fate of their people.

"Release the energy," he commanded, his voice steady despite the turmoil raging within him.

With a single gesture from Illana, the crystals flared to life, their light exploding outward in a brilliant, blinding burst of energy that seemed to consume the very air around them. The ground beneath them trembled as the power surged through the Citadel, racing upward and outward toward the Draco fleet.

In an instant, the dark ships were engulfed in the wave of energy, their weapons silenced, their engines flickering as the power of the crystals overwhelmed their systems. For a moment, the sky itself seemed to glow with the light of the Lyran crystals, as if the very essence of the planet was reaching out to push back the darkness.

But even as the Dracos faltered, the Lyrans knew that this was only a temporary victory. The energy released by the crystals had bought them time—nothing more.

As the light began to fade, Kallaris turned to his people, his expression grim but determined. "We must evacuate," he said, his voice calm but filled with urgency. "Our world cannot be saved, but our legacy can. We will carry the light of Lyra with us into the stars."

And so, as the Draco ships flickered and began to fall back, the Lyrans prepared to leave their home. The beautiful world of Lyra, with its twin suns and crystalline cities, was now a memory—a beacon of light that would live on in the hearts of its people as they journeyed toward their new destiny.

Chapter 2: Shadows on the Horizon

Lyra had always been a sanctuary—a world bathed in the light of two suns, shielded from the chaos that roamed the far reaches of the galaxy. But now, in the wake of the Dracos' initial assault, the very essence of this sanctuary had begun to fray. The Lyrans, once beings of pure light and energy, now found themselves preparing for an uncertain future. The beauty of their world, so long unmarred by conflict, was slowly being overshadowed by the dark forces that sought to claim it.

As the evacuation efforts commenced, the Lyrans moved through their cities in solemn silence. The crystal spires that had once symbolized their connection to the cosmos now stood as reminders of all that they were leaving behind. These structures, shaped by the energies of the universe itself, had been their home for countless millennia. Now, they would soon be abandoned, left to crumble in the aftermath of the inevitable destruction.

Elder Kallaris walked among his people, his luminous form dimmed by the weight of the responsibility that now rested on his shoulders. He had made the decision to release the energy of the crystals, buying them precious time, but he knew that time was fleeting. The Dracos would recover. They always did. And when they did, they would return with even greater force.

The air was thick with anticipation, but it was also filled with something else—an undercurrent of loss. The Lyrans were not simply fleeing a planet; they were leaving behind a way of life, a philosophy that had shaped their very existence. For as long as anyone could remember, the Lyrans had lived in peace, guided by the belief that the universe itself was a living, breathing entity with which they were intrinsically connected. To leave Lyra was to sever that connection, and for many, the thought of such a break was almost unbearable.

Yet there was no other choice.

At the Crystal Citadel, Maestra Illana remained at the helm of the evacuation efforts, her hands glowing softly as she coordinated the movement of their people. Around her, engineers and scholars worked tirelessly, gathering what knowledge and resources they could carry with them into the stars. They knew they could not take everything, but the core of their civilization—their wisdom, their art, their understanding of the universe—would survive, carried in the minds and hearts of the Lyrans who would live on.

Varaen, ever the philosopher, stood at Illana's side, his mind racing with thoughts of what lay ahead. He had always believed that the Lyrans' destiny was tied to the stars, that their existence had a purpose beyond the boundaries of their home world. But now, as he watched the evacuation unfold, he wondered if that purpose had been one of preservation all along. Perhaps they were not meant to fight the Dracos, but to endure—to carry the light of their knowledge through the darkness and into the future.

"Do you think we'll ever return?" Varaen asked quietly, his voice barely audible above the hum of the crystals.

Illana did not look up from her work. "No," she replied simply. "Lyra's time has passed. The universe has other plans for us now."

Her words, though spoken without emotion, carried a finality that echoed in Varaen's heart. He knew she was right. The Lyrans had always believed that their existence was part of a larger cosmic cycle, and now that cycle was turning. Lyra, once a beacon of peace and enlightenment, was being drawn into the shadow of the Dracos, and there was nothing they could do to stop it.

But even as they prepared to leave, the Lyrans knew that their story was not over. It would continue, though it would take on a new form—one shaped by the unknown, by the journey that lay ahead.

The evacuation was a delicate process, one that required both precision and speed. The Lyrans, with their advanced understanding of energy and technology, had developed ships that could traverse the stars with ease, their propulsion systems powered by the very same crystals that had sustained their planet. These ships, sleek and elegant in design, were now being loaded with the most precious cargo of all—the Lyran people and the knowledge they carried.

Varaen watched as the first of the ships began to lift off, their smooth forms rising gracefully into the sky. He couldn't help but feel a pang of sorrow as he watched them leave. Lyra, with all its beauty and peace, was about to become a memory—a distant echo of a time when balance and harmony ruled their lives.

As he stood there, lost in thought, Elder Kallaris approached him, his presence calm but heavy with the gravity of the moment.

"You seem troubled, Varaen," Kallaris said softly, his glowing eyes reflecting the faint light of the departing ships.

"I am," Varaen admitted. "I keep wondering if there was something more we could have done. Something that could have prevented this."

Kallaris placed a hand on his shoulder, the warmth of his energy a small comfort in the face of such overwhelming loss. "You're not alone in that thought. We all feel it. But we must remember that we are not the architects of this destruction. The Dracos have chosen this path, and we cannot change their nature. All we can do is ensure that our legacy survives."

Varaen nodded, though the weight of his thoughts still lingered. "And what of the Dracos? When they return, what will they find here? Ruins? A world stripped of its energy?"

Kallaris sighed, his form dimming slightly as he spoke. "They will find what they seek—a world drained of its power. The crystals are nearly spent. Once we leave, there will be nothing left for them here. But that does not mean they will stop. The Dracos are relentless. If they cannot have Lyra, they will seek another source of power. It is their nature."

Varaen frowned, his thoughts racing. "And if they come after us?"

"Then we will be ready," Kallaris replied, his voice filled with quiet determination. "We may have lost Lyra, but we have not lost ourselves. The light of our civilization still burns within each of us. The Dracos may be powerful, but they cannot extinguish that light. We will endure."

The words brought a measure of comfort to Varaen, though the reality of their situation still weighed heavily on his heart. The Lyrans had always believed in the power of peace, in the strength of unity with the universe. But now, they were facing an enemy who cared nothing for such things. The Dracos were beings of pure conquest, their hunger for power insatiable. And as long as they existed, the Lyrans would never truly be free.

But for now, all they could do was focus on survival. Lyra was lost, but the Lyran people were not. They would carry the legacy of their world with them, even if they had to travel to the farthest reaches of the galaxy to do so.

As the evacuation continued, the Lyrans worked tirelessly to ensure that every soul and every piece of vital knowledge was safely aboard the ships. The Crystal Citadel, once a place of reflection and peace, had become a hub of frantic activity. Crystals were carefully loaded into secure containers, ancient texts and artifacts were gathered, and the most gifted scholars and philosophers were assigned to the evacuation ships.

Despite the flurry of movement, there was a solemn silence that hung over the citadel. The Lyrans, even in their urgency, were aware that they were witnessing the end of an era. Every crystal, every artifact, every piece of knowledge that was loaded onto the ships was a reminder of what they were leaving behind. It was a reminder that Lyra, with all its beauty and grace, would soon be nothing more than a memory.

Illana moved through the citadel with quiet efficiency, her mind focused on the task at hand. She had been entrusted with overseeing the evacuation, and she would see it through, no matter the cost. But as she passed by the great crystalline pillars that lined the halls of the citadel, she couldn't help but feel a deep sense of loss. These pillars, like the rest of Lyra, had been a part of her life for as long as she could remember. Now, they would soon be gone, reduced to rubble when the Dracos returned to claim what was left.

"We cannot save everything," she whispered to herself, her voice barely audible above the hum of the crystals. "But we can save enough."

Her thoughts were interrupted by a sudden surge of energy from the crystals. It was faint, barely noticeable to the untrained eye, but Illana, as the Keeper of the Crystals, felt it immediately. She stopped in her tracks, her glowing eyes narrowing as she focused on the energy signature.

It was a warning.

The crystals, connected as they were to the cosmic energies of the universe, were sending out a signal—an alert that something was coming. Something powerful.

Without hesitation, Illana made her way to the central chamber of the citadel, where Elder Kallaris and the other Council members were gathered. She arrived just as Kallaris was issuing his final orders for the evacuation, his calm voice guiding the remaining Lyrans through the process.

"Kallaris," Illana said, her voice urgent. "The crystals have detected something. The Dracos are approaching."

Kallaris turned to her, his expression grave. "How long do we have?"

"Minutes," she replied. "Maybe less. We need to hurry."

The Council members exchanged worried glances, but there was no panic. They had prepared for this. They knew the Dracos would return, and they had done everything in their power to ensure the evacuation would be completed before that happened.

"Then we must finish what we started," Kallaris said firmly. "We cannot allow the Dracos to take what we've built."

As the final ships were loaded and prepared for departure, a palpable tension settled over the citadel. The Lyrans, despite their calm exteriors, could feel the weight of the moment pressing down on them. The Dracos were closing in, and time was running out.

Illana worked swiftly, guiding the last of the crystal containers onto the ships. The crystals, the heart of Lyra's energy and wisdom, were their most valuable asset. Without them, the Lyrans would be cut off from the cosmic forces that had shaped their civilization. But with them, there was hope—hope that they could rebuild, that they could survive.

"All ships are ready for departure," Varaen said as he approached Illana, his voice steady despite the urgency of the situation. "The Council has boarded the lead ship. We're the last to leave."

Illana nodded, her mind racing as she made one final check of the energy fields surrounding the crystals. "Everything is secure," she said. "Let's go."

The two of them made their way to the final evacuation ship, their forms glowing faintly in the dim light of the citadel. As they stepped aboard, they took one last look at the world they were leaving behind.

Lyra, with its twin suns and shimmering cities, was still beautiful. But that beauty was fleeting. The Dracos were coming, and soon, all that would remain of this world would be ash and ruins.

Inside the ship, Elder Kallaris was waiting. His expression was calm, but there was a sadness in his eyes that could not be hidden.

"It's time," he said quietly. "We must go."

With a nod, Varaen and Illana took their places alongside him. The ship's engines hummed to life, and within moments, they were lifting off, leaving the Crystal Citadel behind.

As the ship ascended into the sky, the Lyrans watched in silence as their home disappeared from view. The cities, the forests, the oceans—all of it was fading into the distance, consumed by the shadow of the approaching Draco fleet.

For a moment, there was nothing but silence. And then, in the distance, they saw it—the first Draco ship breaking through the clouds, its dark form a stark contrast to the light of Lyra's twin suns.

"They've arrived," Varaen whispered, his voice filled with both fear and resolve.

Kallaris closed his eyes, his form glowing softly as he whispered a silent farewell to the world he had called home for so long. "May the light of Lyra live on in us," he said quietly. "And may we find a new home among the stars."

The Lyran evacuation fleet moved silently through the atmosphere, their ships gliding effortlessly toward the vast expanse of space. Below them, the surface of Lyra was a patchwork of shimmering cities and pristine landscapes, a world untouched by war or conflict—until now.

The Dracos had arrived in full force. Their ships, dark and menacing, descended upon the planet like predators closing in on their prey. The Lyrans watched from the safety of their ships, their hearts heavy with the knowledge that Lyra, the world they had nurtured and protected for so long, was about to fall.

Inside the lead ship, Elder Kallaris stood at the viewing port, his glowing eyes fixed on the sight below. He could see the Draco ships as they descended upon the Crystal Citadel, their weapons primed and ready to strike. It was a sight that filled him with both sorrow and anger—sorrow for the world they were leaving behind, and anger for the senseless destruction that was about to unfold.

"We did all we could," Illana said softly, standing beside him. "Lyra may be lost, but our people are not."

Kallaris nodded, though the weight of the moment still pressed heavily on his heart. "I know," he said quietly. "But it does not make it any easier to watch."

The ship's engines hummed as they broke free from the planet's atmosphere, entering the vast, dark void of space. Ahead of them lay the stars—distant, cold, and filled with the promise of both danger and hope. The Lyrans knew that their journey was only just beginning. They were leaving behind everything they had ever known, but they were not leaving behind their purpose. The light of Lyra, the wisdom of their civilization, would live on in them, carried forward into the unknown.

"We will rebuild," Varaen said, his voice filled with quiet determination. "We will find a new home, and we will carry the legacy of Lyra with us."

Kallaris turned to him, a small smile forming on his lips. "Yes," he said softly. "We will."

And so, as the Draco ships descended upon Lyra, the Lyrans left their home behind. The twin suns of Lyra, once symbols of peace and harmony, now shone down upon a world that was about to be consumed by darkness.

But the Lyrans would not be consumed. They would endure. They would survive. And as they journeyed into the stars, they carried with them the light of a world that had once been a beacon of peace and wisdom—a light that would guide them to whatever lay ahead.

Chapter 3: The First Signs Of Ruin

Lyran Legacy: The Starseed Chronicles Begin

As the Lyran fleet sailed silently through the dark expanse of space, their ships gliding effortlessly between the stars, there was a collective sense of loss that filled the hearts of every Lyran aboard. Lyra, their beautiful, radiant home, was now behind them—a world that had existed in perfect harmony for millennia, now under the shadow of destruction. For the first time in their long history, the Lyrans found themselves adrift, not only in the physical sense but in a deeper, more spiritual way. They were no longer tied to their beloved planet, and the reality of that loss was only just beginning to settle in.

Elder Kallaris sat in quiet meditation in the observation chamber of the lead ship, his eyes closed as he reached out with his consciousness, seeking some sense of peace in the wake of their departure. The stars, cold and distant, provided little comfort. Though the Lyrans had always been connected to the cosmos, their connection to Lyra had been the strongest of all, and now that bond had been severed.

The ship was silent save for the faint hum of the crystals powering its systems. The other Lyrans aboard, sensing the gravity of the moment, moved quietly through the halls, their normally radiant forms dimmed by the weight of their emotions. It was as though the light of Lyra had gone out inside them, leaving only a faint glow to remind them of the brilliance that had once been.

As Kallaris meditated, he felt the presence of Varaen enter the room. The younger Lyran, always so filled with questions and curiosity, had been quiet since their departure, his mind clearly preoccupied with thoughts of what lay ahead.

"Kallaris," Varaen said softly, breaking the silence. "May I join you?"

Without opening his eyes, Kallaris nodded. "Of course."

Varaen sat beside him, his form flickering faintly in the dim light of the chamber. For a long moment, neither of them spoke, content to sit in the quietude of space, surrounded by the distant glow of the stars. But eventually, Varaen's thoughts bubbled to the surface, unable to be contained any longer.

"Do you think we made the right decision?" he asked, his voice heavy with uncertainty.

Kallaris opened his eyes, gazing out at the vast expanse before them. "I do not know," he replied honestly. "The universe is vast, and its currents are difficult to predict. We followed the path that we believed was best for our people. Whether it was the right path... only time will tell."

Varaen nodded, though the elder's words did little to ease the uncertainty gnawing at his mind. "I cannot stop thinking about what we left behind," he admitted. "The knowledge, the beauty, the peace... it feels as though we abandoned it all. And for what? A future we cannot see?"

Kallaris turned to him, his gaze soft but steady. "We did not abandon our past, Varaen. We carry it with us. The knowledge, the beauty, the peace—they are not tied to Lyra. They are a part of us. As long as we live, the legacy of Lyra will endure. Our journey is not about leaving behind what we were, but about preserving it, carrying it forward into whatever lies ahead."

Varaen considered this for a moment, his eyes drifting to the stars beyond the window. "But what if the Dracos find us again? What if we can never escape them?"

Kallaris sighed softly. "The Dracos are a force unlike any we have ever encountered. Their hunger for power knows no bounds. But we are not powerless. We carry the light of Lyra within us, and as long as we remain true to our purpose, they cannot destroy us. They may take our world, but they cannot take our spirit."

It was a comforting thought, but Varaen still felt the weight of doubt pressing down on him. The Dracos had already proven their might, and the Lyrans had barely escaped with their lives. What hope did they have of avoiding such a relentless enemy forever?

As if sensing Varaen's inner turmoil, Kallaris placed a hand on his shoulder. "We cannot predict the future, Varaen. But we can shape it. We have the knowledge and the wisdom of countless generations behind us. And we have each other. That is more than enough."

Varaen smiled faintly, though the uncertainty in his heart remained. "I hope you're right, Kallaris," he said softly. "I hope you're right."

While Kallaris and Varaen pondered the uncertainties of their future, Maestra Illana stood in the heart of the ship's crystal chamber, her hands gently tracing the surface of the glowing stones that powered the vessel. The crystals were humming softly, their energy in perfect harmony with the ship's systems, but Illana could sense something beneath the surface—an unease, a subtle disturbance that had not been there before.

She had always been deeply attuned to the crystals, able to sense their moods and energies with a precision that few others could match. And now, as they traveled farther from Lyra, she could feel the crystals changing. It was as if their connection to the cosmic currents had been disrupted, their once-steady flow of energy becoming more erratic, more difficult to control.

Illana frowned, her fingers moving delicately across the surface of one of the largest crystals in the chamber. "What is happening to you?" she murmured, her voice barely above a whisper.

The crystals, of course, did not answer. But Illana could feel their distress. It was as though they were reacting to something in the space around them, something unseen but powerful. She closed her eyes, reaching out with her mind to try and understand the source of the disturbance.

It didn't take long for her to realize what it was.

The Dracos.

Even though they were now far from Lyra, the presence of the Dracos could still be felt in the energy fields that surrounded them. Their dark, malevolent force was like a shadow, lingering just beyond the reach of the Lyrans, but ever-present, a constant reminder of the danger that pursued them.

Illana opened her eyes, her heart heavy with the realization. The Dracos were not just a physical threat—they were an energetic one. Their presence, their very existence, disrupted the natural balance of the universe, and now that imbalance was spreading, infecting the crystals themselves.

"We are not free of them," she whispered, her voice trembling with the weight of the truth. "They follow us, even now."

Without hesitation, Illana left the crystal chamber and made her way to the ship's command center, where Kallaris and the other Council members were gathered. She entered the room with an urgency that immediately caught their attention.

"The crystals are changing," she said without preamble. "I can feel it. The Dracos' presence is affecting them, even from this distance. Their energy is disrupting the balance, and I fear that if we do not find a way to counter it, the crystals will fail."

Kallaris frowned, his eyes narrowing as he considered her words. "The crystals are our lifeblood," he said slowly. "If they fail, we lose everything. We must find a way to protect them."

Illana nodded, her expression grave. "I have been thinking about this since we left Lyra. The crystals are tied to the cosmic energy of the universe, but they are also deeply connected to us. Perhaps, if we strengthen our own energy fields, we can stabilize the crystals, protect them from the influence of the Dracos."

"It's worth a try," Varaen said, stepping forward. "We have nothing to lose."

The Council members exchanged glances, their expressions serious but determined. They had survived the destruction of their home world, and now they faced a new challenge—

one that would test not just their knowledge, but their very connection to the universe itself.

The Lyrans gathered in the ship's central chamber, their luminous forms flickering faintly as they prepared for what could be their most difficult test yet. The crystals, though stable for now, had begun to show signs of strain under the influence of the Dracos' dark energy. Illana's proposal was their only hope—to use their own energy fields to reinforce the crystals, to protect them from the corruption that threatened to spread through the fleet.

Elder Kallaris stood at the center of the chamber, his calm presence a source of reassurance for the Lyrans gathered around him. Despite the uncertainty of the situation, there was a quiet strength in the air, a sense of purpose that had not wavered even in the face of so much loss.

"We are Lyrans," Kallaris said, his voice steady but filled with quiet intensity. "We are more than our world, more than the crystals that have sustained us. We are connected to the universe in ways that no other race can understand. And now, we must use that connection to protect what remains of our civilization."

The Lyrans nodded in agreement, their forms glowing faintly as they prepared to focus their energy. Illana stood at the edge of the circle, her hands resting gently on the largest of the crystals, her eyes closed as she tuned herself to the subtle vibrations of the energy fields around her.

"We must be in perfect harmony," she said softly. "The crystals will respond to us, but only if we are united in our purpose. Focus on the light within you—the light of Lyra, the light that has always guided us. Let it flow through you and into the crystals. Together, we can protect them."

The Lyrans, ever attuned to the flow of energy, began to concentrate, their forms becoming brighter as they focused their collective will on the task at hand. The chamber was filled with a soft, radiant glow as their energy fields expanded, reaching out to touch the crystals that powered their ship.

For a long moment, there was only silence—the kind of deep, profound silence that comes when all things are in perfect alignment. And then, slowly, the crystals began to hum, their energy fields stabilizing as the Lyrans' light flowed into them. The dissonance that Illana had sensed earlier was fading, replaced by a gentle harmony that filled the air with a sense of peace and balance.

"It's working," Illana said softly, her eyes still closed as she focused on maintaining the flow of energy. "We are stabilizing them."

But even as she spoke, she knew that this was only a temporary solution. The Dracos' influence was too strong, too pervasive to be countered for long. Sooner or later, they would have to face the reality that the crystals alone could not protect them forever.

For now, though, they had bought themselves more time.

The process of stabilizing the crystals took longer than expected, but when it was finally complete, there was a palpable sense of relief that swept through the Lyran fleet. The immediate threat had been averted, and for the moment, their ships were once again functioning at full capacity. But the relief was tempered by the knowledge that this was only a temporary reprieve. The Dracos were still out there, their dark energy an ever-present threat that could not be ignored.

In the aftermath of the ritual, Kallaris gathered the Council once more to discuss their next steps. The ship's central chamber was filled with the soft hum of the stabilized crystals, but the mood was somber. The Lyrans knew that they could not continue like this indefinitely. They needed to find a new home—a place where they could rebuild, far from the reach of the Dracos.

"We cannot wander the stars forever," Kallaris said, his voice steady but filled with the weight of the situation. "We need to find a world where we can settle, where we can rebuild what we have lost."

The Council members nodded in agreement, though the question of where they could go remained unanswered. The galaxy was vast, filled with countless worlds, but most of them were either uninhabitable or already claimed by other civilizations. And with the Dracos pursuing them, they would need to find a place where they could hide, where the darkness of their enemy could not reach them.

"I have been scanning the star charts," Varaen said, stepping forward. "There is a system on the edge of the galaxy—far from any known trade routes or established civilizations. It is remote, isolated, but there is a planet there. One that could potentially sustain life."

Kallaris turned to him, his expression thoughtful. "And do you believe the Dracos would follow us there?"

Varaen shook his head. "It is unlikely. The system is too far from their usual path of conquest. If we can reach it, we may have a chance to build a new life there—at least for a time."

The Council members exchanged glances, their expressions a mixture of hope and caution. It was a risk, but they had little choice. The longer they remained in the open, the more vulnerable they became. If they were to survive, they needed to find a sanctuary—a new home where they could live in peace, free from the shadow of the Dracos.

"Then it is decided," Kallaris said, his voice filled with quiet resolve. "We will make for this system. Let us hope the stars guide us safely there."

The Lyran fleet adjusted its course, setting a path for the distant star system that Varaen had identified. The journey would take time—weeks, perhaps months—but the Lyrans were patient. They had always understood the importance of the long view, of thinking in terms of generations rather than moments. And now, as they sailed through the dark expanse of space, they knew that their survival depended on their ability to adapt to the unknown.

As the days passed, the Lyrans settled into a routine. The initial shock of losing their home had begun to fade, replaced by a quiet determination to rebuild. Though they had left Lyra behind, they carried its legacy with them—the knowledge, the wisdom, the light of their civilization.

Varaen spent his days in the ship's observatory, studying the star charts and calculating their progress. The system they were heading toward was remote, but it held promise. The planet, though largely unexplored, was believed to be rich in natural resources, with a climate that could potentially support life. It was not Lyra, but it was a start.

Illana, meanwhile, continued to monitor the crystals, ensuring that they remained stable as the fleet traveled through the void. Though the Dracos' influence was still faintly present, the ritual they had performed had strengthened the crystals' defenses, giving them a buffer against the dark energy that threatened to corrupt them.

Kallaris, ever the leader, spent his time among the people, offering words of comfort and guidance. Though the journey was long and uncertain, he reminded them that they were not alone. The Lyrans were a people of light, connected to the cosmos in ways that no other race could understand. And as long as they remained true to themselves, they would find their way.

As the fleet moved closer to the distant system, there was a growing sense of hope among the Lyrans. The stars, once cold and distant, now seemed to offer a glimmer of possibility. The path ahead was still unclear, but for the first time since leaving Lyra, there was a feeling that they were moving toward something—not just away from the destruction that had claimed their home, but toward a new future, one filled with potential.

"We will rebuild," Kallaris had said, and the Lyrans believed him. They would carry the light of Lyra into the stars, and no matter what lay ahead, they would endure.

The Dracos may have taken their world, but they had not taken their spirit.

Chapter 4: The Battle for Lyra Begins

Far behind the Lyran fleet, Lyra itself had become a battleground. The once-pristine world, with its twin suns and crystalline cities, now stood on the brink of annihilation. The Draco fleet descended upon it like a storm, their dark ships blotting out the light of the suns, casting long shadows across the land. To the Dracos, Lyra was more than just a planet; it was a prize—a world rich with energy, a source of unimaginable power that could fuel their conquest of the galaxy.

Tzaroth, the Draco warlord, stood at the helm of his flagship, his eyes fixed on the planet below. His face, cold and expressionless, betrayed none of the excitement that roiled within him. This was the moment he had been waiting for—the culmination of his long campaign to seize the energy crystals of Lyra. He knew that if he succeeded here, the balance of power in the galaxy would shift forever in favor of the Dracos.

"The Lyrans have fled," one of his officers reported, his voice a low, guttural rasp. "Their fleet is no longer within the system. The planet is undefended."

Tzaroth's lips curled into a cruel smile. "Fools. They should have stayed and fought. Now their world belongs to us."

He turned to his second-in-command, a tall, imposing figure clad in dark armor. "Prepare the landing parties. I want the Crystal Citadel secured immediately. Once we control the crystals, no force in the galaxy will be able to stop us."

The officer bowed low and hurried to carry out the command. Tzaroth, meanwhile, returned his gaze to Lyra, his eyes narrowing as he studied the planet's surface. He could sense the immense power hidden beneath its surface, the raw energy of the crystals that had sustained the Lyrans for millennia. It was a power unlike anything he had ever encountered—a power that, once harnessed, would make the Dracos unstoppable.

But even as the Draco ships began their descent, the planet seemed to resist. The energy fields surrounding the Crystal Citadel flared to life, shimmering in the atmosphere like a barrier of light. Though the Lyrans had fled, they had left behind powerful defenses, and those defenses were now fighting back.

"Energy fields detected around the Citadel," the officer reported, his voice tinged with frustration. "It appears the Lyrans anticipated our arrival."

Tzaroth's smile faded, replaced by a look of cold calculation. "It makes no difference. Their defenses will not hold for long. Increase power to the disruptors. I want those fields down."

The Draco fleet responded immediately, their ships unleashing a barrage of dark energy beams that slammed into the Lyran defenses with devastating force. The energy fields shimmered and flickered under the onslaught, but they held—at least for the moment.

Tzaroth watched with grim satisfaction as the battle unfolded. He had no doubt that the Lyran defenses would eventually crumble. It was only a matter of time.

Inside the Crystal Citadel, the remnants of Lyra's defense systems worked tirelessly to maintain the energy shield that protected the planet's most sacred site. Though the Lyrans had fled, their technology remained, and it was now the only thing standing between the Dracos and total domination.

The Citadel's automated systems hummed with activity, directing power from the remaining crystals into the energy fields that surrounded the structure. But even with the full power of the Citadel's crystals at their disposal, the Lyran defenses were not invincible. The Dracos' relentless assault was taking its toll, and the energy fields were beginning to weaken.

Deep within the Citadel, in a chamber that had once been the heart of Lyran spiritual life, a lone figure moved through the shadows. **Varael**, one of the few Lyrans who had remained behind when the evacuation began, had taken it upon himself to ensure that the Citadel's defenses held as long as possible. He had been one of the Lyran scholars tasked with safeguarding their knowledge, and now, in the absence of the Council, he had chosen to stay behind to protect what remained of their civilization.

Varael was no warrior, but he was wise, and he understood the power of the crystals better than most. He knew that if the Dracos gained control of the Citadel, they would not only harness its energy but also its knowledge—knowledge that could be used to devastate entire star systems. And so, he had stayed behind, a silent guardian in the midst of the chaos.

As he moved through the ancient halls of the Citadel, Varael could feel the energy fields weakening. The crystals, though powerful, were not limitless. They had been designed to work in harmony with the Lyran people, not to fend off a full-scale invasion. Without the Lyrans to guide their power, the crystals were slowly losing their ability to maintain the defenses.

Varael paused in front of a large, glowing crystal that stood at the center of the chamber. Its light was dimmer than it had been when the evacuation began, a clear sign that the energy reserves were running low. He placed his hands on the crystal, closing his eyes as he reached out with his mind, trying to stabilize the flow of energy.

For a moment, the crystal's light brightened, and the energy fields outside the Citadel flared in response, holding back the Dracos for a little longer. But Varael knew it wouldn't be enough. The Dracos were too powerful, their technology too advanced. The Citadel's defenses were doomed to fail.

Still, he couldn't give up. As long as he lived, as long as the crystals still held even a fraction of their power, he would fight to protect Lyra's legacy. He had no illusions about surviving this battle, but that didn't matter. What mattered was ensuring that the Dracos never claimed the power of the crystals.

Outside the Citadel, the battle raged on. The Draco fleet, relentless in its assault, poured wave after wave of dark energy into the Lyran defenses. Each strike chipped away at the energy fields, weakening them further, until finally, with a deafening crack, the first section of the shield collapsed.

Tzaroth, watching from the bridge of his flagship, allowed himself a small smile. "The shield is failing," he said, his voice a low growl of satisfaction. "It won't be long now."

The Dracos intensified their attack, focusing all their firepower on the weakened section of the shield. Within moments, another section of the barrier collapsed, and then another. The Citadel's defenses were crumbling, and soon, the entire structure would be exposed.

"Prepare the landing parties," Tzaroth commanded. "Once the shield is down, we will take the Citadel by force. Leave nothing standing."

The Draco ships descended, their dark forms casting long shadows across the planet's surface as they prepared for the final assault. Tzaroth's soldiers, clad in their fearsome black armor, stood ready to storm the Citadel and claim its treasures for the Draco Empire.

But even as the shield continued to fall, Varael did not give up. Inside the Citadel, he worked tirelessly to reroute power from the remaining crystals, doing everything he could to keep the defenses intact. He knew it was a losing battle, but he had no other choice. If the Dracos took the Citadel, all hope for the Lyran people would be lost.

With each passing moment, the energy fields grew weaker. The crystals, their power drained by the constant assault, began to dim, their once-brilliant light fading into darkness. Varael could feel their energy slipping away, like sand through his fingers.

In a final, desperate attempt, Varael reached out with his mind, tapping into the deepest reserves of the crystals' power. He felt the energy surge through him, filling him with a sense of connection to the universe that he had never experienced before. For a brief moment, the Citadel's defenses flared back to life, and the Dracos' assault was halted.

But the effort was too much. The crystals, already weakened, could not sustain the surge for long. With a final, shuddering pulse, the energy fields collapsed entirely, leaving the Citadel vulnerable.

Varael staggered back, his body trembling from the effort. He had given everything he had, but it hadn't been enough. The Dracos would take the Citadel, and with it, the last remnants of Lyra's power.

The Draco landing parties wasted no time. As soon as the shield collapsed, they descended upon the Citadel like vultures, their black armor gleaming in the faint light of the crystals. Their orders were clear—destroy everything and take whatever they could. The Citadel was to be stripped of its energy, its knowledge, and its treasures.

Tzaroth, watching from his flagship, felt a surge of triumph. Lyra, the jewel of the galaxy, was now his. The Lyrans had fled, leaving their precious world undefended, and now he would claim its power for himself. With the energy of the crystals at his command, there would be nothing to stop the Draco Empire.

As the Draco soldiers stormed the Citadel, Varael retreated deeper into the structure, his mind racing as he tried to come up with a plan. He had no weapons, no way to fight back against the invaders, but he knew that the Citadel still held one final secret—one that the Dracos did not yet know about.

In the deepest chamber of the Citadel, hidden away from even the most powerful Lyran leaders, lay the **Core Crystal**—the heart of the Citadel's power. It was larger than any of the other crystals, its energy more ancient and more powerful than anything the Dracos could imagine. If Varael could reach the Core Crystal, there might still be a way to stop the Dracos from claiming the Citadel's power.

With a sense of urgency driving him, Varael made his way through the crumbling halls of the Citadel, the sound of the Draco soldiers growing louder behind him. He knew that time was running out. If he didn't reach the Core Crystal soon, it would be too late.

The chamber that housed the Core Crystal was hidden deep within the Citadel, accessible only through a series of concealed passageways that few Lyrans even knew existed. Varael, as one of the scholars entrusted with the knowledge of the Citadel, knew the way. But the path was long, and the Dracos were closing in.

Finally, after what felt like an eternity, Varael reached the chamber. The doors, massive and carved from the same crystal as the Citadel itself, glowed faintly in the dim light. With a deep breath, Varael placed his hands on the doors, using the last of his energy to open them.

The chamber beyond was vast, its walls lined with intricate patterns of light and energy. And at the center of the room, bathed in a soft, otherworldly glow, stood the **Core Crystal**.

The Core Crystal was unlike any other crystal in the Citadel. Its surface was smooth and flawless, its light pulsing with a steady, rhythmic energy that filled the chamber with a sense of calm and power. Varael approached it slowly, his heart racing as he considered what he was about to do.

The Core Crystal held the key to the Citadel's power, but it also held a terrible secret. In times of great crisis, the Core could be activated to release all of its energy in one final, cataclysmic burst—a last resort that would destroy not only the Citadel but everything within a vast radius. It was a weapon of unimaginable power, one that the Lyrans had hoped they would never have to use.

But now, with the Dracos closing in, Varael knew that he had no choice. If the Dracos took the Core Crystal, they would wield its power to enslave entire star systems. The only way to stop them was to destroy the Citadel—and himself—along with it.

Varael placed his hands on the surface of the Core Crystal, feeling its energy flow through him. The connection was immediate, powerful, and overwhelming. He could feel the pulse of the universe itself in the crystal, the raw, untamed power that had sustained the Lyrans for millennia.

"I'm sorry," he whispered, his voice trembling with emotion. "But I cannot let you fall into their hands."

With a deep breath, Varael activated the Core Crystal. The chamber filled with light, a brilliant, blinding glow that radiated outward in all directions. The walls of the Citadel trembled as the energy built to a crescendo, and Varael closed his eyes, knowing that this was the end.

Outside, the Dracos had begun to breach the Citadel's inner defenses, their soldiers storming through the halls with ruthless efficiency. But as they neared the chamber that housed the Core Crystal, they felt it—a surge of energy so powerful that it shook the ground beneath their feet.

Tzaroth, watching from his flagship, sensed the shift immediately. "What is happening?" he demanded, his voice filled with anger.

"Energy spike detected from within the Citadel," one of his officers reported. "It's… it's off the charts, my lord. We've never seen anything like it."

Tzaroth's eyes widened as he realized what was happening. The Lyrans, in their final act of defiance, were destroying the Citadel. And with it, any hope of claiming the power of the crystals.

"Pull back!" Tzaroth roared. "Get the soldiers out of there! Now!"

But it was too late.

With a final, blinding flash of light, the Core Crystal released its full power. The explosion was immense, tearing through the Citadel and sending shockwaves across the planet's surface. The Draco soldiers were vaporized in an instant, their ships thrown from the sky by the force of the blast.

Lyra, once a beacon of peace and harmony, was no more.

In the silence that followed, the remnants of the Draco fleet limped away from the system, their hopes of conquest shattered. And in the cold expanse of space, the Lyran fleet sailed onward, unaware of the sacrifice that had just been made to protect their legacy.

Lyra was gone, but its light would live on in the hearts of its people.

Chapter 5: The Fall of Lyra

The explosion of the Core Crystal marked the end of Lyra. The energy unleashed in that final act of defiance tore through the planet, reducing the once-beautiful world to a wasteland of shattered cities and scorched landscapes. The twin suns, which had once bathed the planet in their golden light, now illuminated only the remnants of what had once been a beacon of peace and harmony. Lyra was gone, and with it, the home of the Lyran people.

For those aboard the Lyran evacuation fleet, the destruction of their world was a silent, invisible horror. Far from the system, they did not witness the moment when the Citadel was consumed by the light of the Core Crystal's final release. They did not see the Draco ships fall from the sky or the Draco soldiers perish in the blinding explosion. But they felt it.

Even across the vast distance of space, the Lyrans felt the moment when Lyra died. It was as if a part of their very being had been torn away, leaving behind only an empty, aching void. The connection they had once shared with their planet, with its energy and its beauty, was gone, severed in an instant. There were no words to describe the loss, no way to capture the depth of the sorrow that now gripped their hearts.

Elder Kallaris stood at the observation deck of the lead ship, staring out into the dark void of space. He had felt the moment when Lyra fell, just as every Lyran aboard the fleet had felt it. The light of their world had been extinguished, and though they were still alive, it felt as though they had lost a part of their soul.

Beside him, Varaen stood in silent contemplation. His usual curiosity and philosophical musings had been replaced by a quiet, heavy grief. He, too, had felt the death of Lyra, and though he had known from the beginning that their world was doomed, the reality of it was almost too much to bear.

"We felt it, didn't we?" Varaen finally said, his voice barely a whisper. "The moment it happened. The moment Lyra... died."

Kallaris nodded slowly, his eyes never leaving the stars. "Yes," he said softly. "We all felt it."

The silence that followed was thick with unspoken emotions. There was nothing either of them could say to ease the pain, no words that could fill the void that Lyra's destruction had left behind. It was as though the entire fleet had fallen into mourning, their light dimmed by the weight of the loss.

"We knew it was coming," Varaen continued, his voice trembling slightly. "But knowing it and feeling it... those are two very different things."

Kallaris turned to him, his gaze soft but filled with the wisdom of his long years. "We did what we had to do," he said quietly. "We saved our people. We saved our knowledge. Lyra may be gone, but its legacy will live on in us."

Varaen nodded, though the words did little to soothe the ache in his heart. He had spent his entire life studying the universe, seeking to understand its mysteries and its wonders. But now, as he stood in the wake of Lyra's destruction, all the knowledge in the galaxy seemed meaningless compared to the loss of his home.

"What do we do now?" Varaen asked, his voice filled with uncertainty. "Where do we go from here?"

Kallaris sighed softly, his shoulders heavy with the burden of leadership. "We move forward," he said, his voice firm despite the sorrow that clung to it. "We carry the light of Lyra with us, and we find a new home. A place where we can rebuild, where we can honor the memory of our world."

Varaen said nothing, but the weight of the elder's words settled over him like a cloak. He knew Kallaris was right. They couldn't dwell in their grief forever. The Lyrans had survived, and as long as they lived, there was hope. But even that knowledge couldn't dispel the darkness that now hung over them, a reminder of the world they had lost.

As the fleet continued its journey through the stars, the Lyrans slowly began to come to terms with their loss. The initial shock of Lyra's destruction had left them reeling, but they were a resilient people, and they knew that they could not remain paralyzed by grief. There was work to be done, and a new future to build.

Inside the lead ship, Maestra Illana worked tirelessly in the crystal chamber, her hands gently tending to the glowing stones that powered the fleet. Though the crystals remained stable, Illana could sense the subtle shifts in their energy. They, too, had felt the death of Lyra, and though they continued to function, their light was not as bright as it once had been.

"It's as if they're grieving with us," Illana murmured to herself as she adjusted the flow of energy through the crystals. "They feel the loss, just as we do."

The crystals had always been deeply connected to the Lyran people, their energy flowing in harmony with the life force of the planet. Now, with Lyra gone, that connection had been severed, and the crystals were struggling to adapt to the new reality. Illana knew that they would need to find a way to stabilize the crystals soon, or the fleet's journey would become even more perilous.

As she worked, Illana felt a presence behind her and turned to see Varaen entering the chamber, his expression somber. "How are the crystals holding up?" he asked, his voice quiet.

"They're stable for now," Illana replied, though her tone carried an undercurrent of concern. "But they're... different. The loss of Lyra has affected them, just as it's affected us. Their energy is more erratic, more difficult to control."

Varaen nodded, his brow furrowing in thought. "We've always known that the crystals were tied to Lyra, but I never realized just how deep that connection was."

"Neither did I," Illana admitted. "But now that Lyra is gone, the crystals are struggling to find their balance. We need to find a way to stabilize them, or we could lose the fleet."

Varaen approached one of the larger crystals, his hand hovering just above its surface. He could feel the subtle vibrations of its energy, the faint pulse that had always

71

been a part of the Lyran way of life. But now, that pulse was uneven, as though the crystal itself was struggling to find its rhythm.

"Do you think it's possible?" Varaen asked, his eyes searching Illana's face. "To stabilize them, I mean."

Illana hesitated for a moment before nodding. "I believe so," she said, though there was a hint of uncertainty in her voice. "But it will take time. The crystals are resilient, but they're also fragile. We need to be careful, or we could cause more harm than good."

Varaen sighed softly, his mind racing with the weight of their situation. They had escaped the destruction of Lyra, but the challenges they faced were far from over. The loss of their world had left them vulnerable, and now, more than ever, they needed to find a way to stabilize their energy and move forward.

"We'll figure it out," Varaen said finally, his voice filled with quiet determination. "We have to."

While Illana and Varaen focused on stabilizing the crystals, the rest of the fleet turned its attention to the future. With Lyra gone, the Lyrans needed to find a new home, a place where they could rebuild their civilization and ensure the survival of their legacy. But the search for such a world was fraught with uncertainty.

The galaxy was vast, and though there were countless planets, few would be suitable for the Lyrans' unique way of life. They needed a world that could sustain not only their physical needs but also their spiritual connection to the cosmos. A world where the crystals could thrive, and where the Lyrans could continue their work as the guardians of knowledge and peace.

Elder Kallaris had tasked the fleet's navigators with scanning the surrounding star systems for any signs of a suitable planet. But so far, their efforts had yielded little. Most of the worlds they encountered were either too inhospitable or already claimed by other civilizations. And with the Dracos still out there, lurking in the shadows, the Lyrans needed a place where they could hide, where they could regroup and recover without fear of being discovered.

Kallaris knew that time was running out. The fleet's resources were limited, and though the Lyrans were skilled at surviving in the harshest of conditions, they could not remain adrift in space forever. They needed a new home, and they needed it soon.

As the search continued, Kallaris found himself spending more and more time in quiet meditation, seeking guidance from the universe. The Lyrans had always believed that the cosmos had a plan, that every star, every planet, every event was part of a greater design. But now, as they drifted through the vastness of space, Kallaris began to question whether that belief still held true.

Had the universe abandoned them? Or was there still a path forward, a future that they had not yet seen?

One night, as Kallaris sat in meditation, he felt something—an almost imperceptible shift in the energy around him. It was faint, like a whisper carried on the wind, but it was enough to stir him from his thoughts.

Opening his eyes, Kallaris focused his mind on the source of the disturbance. It was far away, somewhere in the distance, but it was there—a faint pulse of energy, different from anything he had felt before.

"Could it be…?" he murmured to himself, his heart quickening with a sudden surge of hope.

Rising to his feet, Kallaris made his way to the command center, where Varaen and the other navigators were still scanning the surrounding systems.

"I've felt something," Kallaris said as he entered the room, his voice filled with quiet excitement. "A disturbance in the energy fields. Something distant, but powerful. We need to investigate."

Varaen and the others exchanged glances, their expressions curious but cautious. "What kind of disturbance?" Varaen asked, his brow furrowed.

"I'm not sure," Kallaris admitted. "But it's different. It feels… alive. Like a signal from the universe itself."

Varaen nodded slowly, his curiosity piqued. "Then we should follow it. If it's as powerful as you say, it could be the lead we've been searching for."

The fleet adjusted its course, following the faint energy signal that Kallaris had detected. It was distant, barely noticeable amid the background noise of the cosmos, but it was there—an unmistakable pulse of energy that seemed to grow stronger as they drew closer. For the first time since leaving Lyra, there was a sense of purpose, of direction. The Lyrans didn't know what they would find, but the very act of searching, of moving toward something, was enough to lift their spirits.

Days passed as the fleet continued its journey, the stars around them shifting as they ventured deeper into unknown territory. The energy signal, though still faint, became more pronounced with each passing day. It was unlike anything the Lyrans had ever encountered, a subtle but persistent presence that seemed to call to them, guiding them forward.

Varaen spent hours studying the signal, analyzing its frequency and trying to determine its origin. But no matter how much data he collected, he couldn't identify the source. It wasn't coming from a star or a planet, and it didn't match any known energy patterns. It was something new, something different—and that only made it more intriguing.

"It's almost as if it's alive," Varaen mused one day as he reviewed the data with Kallaris. "The way the signal pulses, the way it changes... it feels organic, like it's responding to us."

Kallaris nodded, his expression thoughtful. "I've sensed the same thing. It's not just a random burst of energy—it has intention behind it. Whatever this is, it's calling to us."

The two of them continued to analyze the data, their excitement tempered by caution. The signal, though promising, could still be dangerous. There was no way of knowing what they would find when they reached its source, and with the Dracos still out there, the Lyrans couldn't afford to take unnecessary risks.

But as the fleet drew closer to the source of the signal, it became clear that they were on the verge of something significant. The energy field surrounding the signal grew stronger, more pronounced, until it was nearly impossible to ignore. It was as if the universe itself was guiding them toward their destination, urging them to keep going.

Finally, after what felt like weeks of traveling, the fleet arrived at the edge of a vast, uncharted star system. The energy signal, which had been growing stronger with each passing day, was now so powerful that it filled the entire sensor array with its presence. It was coming from a planet—a distant, isolated world that orbited a single star at the outermost edge of the galaxy.

"There," Varaen said, pointing to the display. "That's where the signal is coming from."

Kallaris studied the planet on the screen, his heart quickening with anticipation. It was a small, rocky world, with a thin atmosphere and a surface dotted with mountains and deep canyons. It wasn't the lush, crystalline paradise that Lyra had been, but there was something about it— something that called to him.

"Set a course for the planet," Kallaris ordered, his voice filled with quiet determination. "We're going down."

Chapter 6: Transformation in Exile, The Arrival

Lyran Legacy: The Starseed Chronicles Begin

The new planet was unlike anything the Lyrans had ever known. It lacked the crystalline beauty of Lyra, the twin suns that had bathed their world in light, and the ethereal harmony they had once taken for granted. But it was alive with energy—a raw, untamed force that surged through the earth and the strange glowing crystals that dotted the planet's surface. As the Lyrans began the slow process of settling into their new home, they could feel the planet reshaping them, as though the very energy of the world was calling for transformation.

Elder Kallaris stood on a high ridge overlooking the expanse of canyons and valleys below. The sky, painted with streaks of orange and violet, was unfamiliar, but it held a strange beauty of its own. The distant star, a single sun much smaller than the ones that had once warmed Lyra, cast long shadows across the land, giving everything an air of mystery and possibility.

Kallaris could feel it—the subtle shift in the energy around him, the way it interacted with his form. The Lyrans, once beings of pure light and energy, were beginning to change. Their forms, which had once been ethereal and fluid, were slowly becoming more solid, more grounded in the physical reality of their new world. It was a transformation that both fascinated and unnerved him.

As he watched the horizon, Varaen approached, his steps quiet but purposeful. The younger Lyran had been studying the planet's energy fields since their arrival, and Kallaris could see the excitement and curiosity in his eyes.

"You feel it too, don't you?" Varaen asked, coming to stand beside Kallaris. "This planet... it's changing us."

Kallaris nodded slowly. "Yes," he said quietly. "I've felt it since we arrived. The energy here is different—more intense, more grounded. It's as though the planet is drawing us into its reality, making us… more physical."

Varaen smiled faintly. "It's not just us. The crystals are changing too. Their energy patterns are different now, more in tune with the planet's own frequencies. I've been studying them, trying to understand the nature of the shift, but it's unlike anything we've encountered before."

Kallaris turned to him, his expression thoughtful. "Do you think it's dangerous?"

"I don't think so," Varaen replied, though there was a hint of uncertainty in his voice. "At least, not yet. The transformation is gradual, almost natural, as if the planet itself is guiding the process. But we need to be careful. This is a new world, with new rules. We can't assume that what worked on Lyra will work here."

Kallaris sighed softly, his gaze returning to the horizon. "Lyra is gone," he said, the weight of the words heavy in the air. "We can never go back to what we were. This planet… this new reality… we must adapt, or we will not survive."

Varaen nodded, though the gravity of Kallaris's words lingered in the air between them. The Lyrans were a people of light, a people who had always existed in harmony with the universe. But now, on this strange and distant world, that harmony was shifting. They were becoming something new—something different. And while the change was subtle for now, both Kallaris and Varaen knew that it was only the beginning.

As the days turned into weeks, the Lyrans settled into their new routines, adapting to the rhythms of their new home. The planet, though harsh and unforgiving in some ways, offered enough resources to sustain them. The glowing crystals that covered the landscape provided energy, much like the ones on Lyra, though their power was wilder, more unpredictable.

Maestra Illana spent much of her time in the heart of the new settlement, working closely with the crystal engineers to understand the properties of the local crystals. Their energy, though similar to the crystals of Lyra, was far more volatile. The crystals pulsed with an intensity that made them difficult to control, but Illana was determined to find a way to harness their power.

"It's as if these crystals are alive in a different way," Illana explained one day to Varaen, who had joined her in the crystal chamber. "They're not just conduits of energy—they seem to respond to the environment, to the changes in the planet's energy fields. I've never seen anything like it."

Varaen examined one of the larger crystals, its surface glowing with a deep, inner light. He could feel the energy pulsing beneath his fingertips, but it was different from what he had known on Lyra. There was a wildness to it, a raw, untamed force that made it both powerful and unpredictable.

"Do you think we can control them?" Varaen asked, his brow furrowed in concentration. "If these crystals are as volatile as they seem, they could be dangerous."

Illana nodded, her face serious. "That's what concerns me. On Lyra, the crystals were stable, their energy perfectly

80

aligned with the natural order of the planet. But here, the crystals are part of a different ecosystem, one we don't fully understand yet. We need to proceed with caution."

The crystal engineers, under Illana's guidance, worked tirelessly to stabilize the energy flows, using what knowledge they had carried from Lyra. But the new crystals resisted their efforts, as though they were unwilling to be tamed by Lyran hands.

Varaen could feel the tension in the air. The Lyrans were trying to recreate the balance they had known on Lyra, but this new world had its own rules, its own rhythms. He wondered if their attempts to impose order on the planet's wild energy might be a mistake.

"Perhaps we need to approach this differently," Varaen said thoughtfully. "Instead of trying to force the crystals into alignment, maybe we need to learn from them. To understand their natural state and work with it, rather than against it."

Illana considered his words, her eyes narrowing as she thought. "You may be right," she said slowly. "This is a new world, and we can't assume that the methods we used on Lyra will work here. We need to adapt to the planet's energy, just as we are adapting physically."

Varaen smiled faintly. "We've always been a people of balance and harmony. Perhaps this planet is teaching us that we need to find a new kind of harmony—one that's more in tune with the wild, untamed forces of this world."

Illana nodded, her face thoughtful. "It won't be easy. But if we can understand this energy, if we can learn to live in harmony with it, then perhaps this world can become our new home."

As the Lyrans worked to understand the energy of their new home, they also began to notice changes in themselves. Their once-ethereal forms, which had shimmered with light and energy, were becoming more solid, more grounded. It was as if the planet's energy was reshaping them, drawing them deeper into its reality.

Varaen was one of the first to notice the change in his own form. His once-glowing skin, which had been almost translucent on Lyra, was now becoming more opaque, more defined. His features, once fluid and shifting, were now sharper, more distinct. He still retained some of the ethereal glow that marked him as a Lyran, but it was fainter now, as though the planet was pulling him closer to the physical world.

He wasn't the only one. All around him, the other Lyrans were undergoing similar transformations. Their bodies were becoming more humanoid, more solid. The change was slow and subtle, but it was undeniable. The Lyrans were no longer the beings of pure energy they had once been.

At first, the transformation was met with concern. The Lyrans had always prided themselves on their connection to the universe, their ability to exist in harmony with the energy fields that flowed through all things. To become more physical, more grounded in the material world, felt like a loss—like a step backward in their spiritual evolution.

But as time passed, the Lyrans began to accept the changes. They understood that this new world was reshaping them, just as they were reshaping it. The transformation was not a loss of their identity, but rather an evolution—a new form of existence that allowed them to adapt to their new environment.

"We are still Lyrans," Kallaris said during one of the gatherings that had become a regular part of their new life. "Our light still burns within us, even if it shines in a different form. We are changing, yes, but we are not losing ourselves. This transformation is a part of our journey, a part of the path that the universe has laid before us."

The others nodded in agreement, though there was still a sense of unease in the air. The Lyrans had always believed that their connection to the universe transcended the physical form, that they were beings of energy and light. To become more human, more grounded in the material world, felt strange—unnatural, even.

But Kallaris's words brought comfort. They were still Lyrans, even if their bodies were changing. Their minds, their spirits, their connection to the greater cosmos remained intact. The light of Lyra still burned within them, even if it had taken on a new shape.

As the Lyrans continued to settle into their new lives, they began to explore more of the planet's surface. The landscape, though rugged and barren in places, held its own unique beauty. Strange plants, unlike anything they had seen on Lyra, grew in the canyons and valleys, their leaves glowing faintly in the light of the distant star. The air was thin but crisp, filled with the scent of unfamiliar flora and the sound of alien winds.

Lyran Legacy: The Starseed Chronicles Begin

Varaen and a group of Lyran explorers ventured deeper into the planet's interior, searching for signs of life or resources that could aid in their survival. The further they traveled, the more they realized that this planet was teeming with energy—raw, untapped energy that pulsed through the ground and the air, radiating from the strange crystals that dotted the landscape.

One day, as the group traveled through a narrow canyon, Varaen stopped in his tracks. He had felt something—a surge of energy, different from the usual pulses of the crystals. It was subtle, almost imperceptible, but it was there, vibrating through the ground beneath his feet.

"Do you feel that?" Varaen asked, turning to the others.

The other explorers paused, their glowing forms flickering slightly as they attuned themselves to the energy of the planet. After a moment, they nodded, their expressions curious.

"It's coming from beneath us," one of them said, his voice filled with wonder. "There's something down there."

Varaen knelt down, placing his hands on the ground. He could feel the energy more clearly now, a steady pulse that seemed to resonate with the crystals around them. It was as though the planet itself was alive, its energy flowing through every rock, every stone, every crystal.

"We need to investigate," Varaen said, rising to his feet. "Whatever is down there, it's important. It's connected to the energy of this planet, and if we can understand it, we might be able to unlock the secrets of this world."

The others nodded in agreement, their curiosity piqued. Together, they began to search for a way to access the underground energy source, their minds racing with the possibilities.

As they explored the canyon, they discovered a narrow fissure in the rock, barely wide enough for a single Lyran to pass through. It led down into the darkness, where the energy pulsed with increasing intensity.

"This is it," Varaen said, his voice filled with excitement. "This is where the energy is coming from."

Without hesitation, Varaen led the way into the fissure, his form glowing faintly as he descended into the depths of the planet. The others followed, their hearts filled with a sense of anticipation.

They didn't know what they would find, but they could feel it—the planet was calling to them, guiding them deeper into its mysteries.

The descent into the planet's interior was slow and treacherous. The narrow fissure twisted and turned, leading the Lyrans deeper and deeper into the darkness. The further they went, the more intense the energy became, vibrating through the walls and floor of the tunnel with a steady, rhythmic pulse.

Finally, after what felt like hours of climbing, they emerged into a vast underground chamber. The air was thick with energy, and the walls of the chamber were lined with massive crystals, each one glowing with a soft, radiant light. It was unlike anything the Lyrans had ever seen—a hidden world, pulsing with the same wild, untamed energy that filled the surface of the planet.

At the center of the chamber stood a massive crystal formation, towering above them like a monument. Its surface was smooth and flawless, and it pulsed with a deep, inner light that seemed to resonate with the very core of the planet.

Varaen approached the formation slowly, his eyes wide with wonder. He could feel the energy radiating from it, a powerful, almost overwhelming force that seemed to connect him to the very heart of the planet.

"This is it," he whispered, his voice filled with awe. "This is the source of the energy we've been feeling."

The other Lyrans gathered around him, their faces filled with the same sense of wonder. The energy in the chamber was palpable, flowing through them like a current, filling them with a sense of connection to the planet that they had never experienced before.

For a long moment, they stood in silence, absorbing the energy, feeling the pulse of the planet beneath their feet. It was as if the planet itself was alive, communicating with them through the crystals, guiding them toward a deeper understanding of its power.

Varaen closed his eyes, allowing the energy to flow through him. He could feel the planet's heartbeat, the steady rhythm of its life force. It was different from Lyra, more raw, more primal, but it was beautiful in its own way.

"We've found it," Varaen said softly. "The heart of this planet. This is what we've been searching for."

The others nodded, their faces filled with a sense of reverence. They had come to this planet seeking a new home, a place where they could rebuild their civilization. But now, standing in the heart of the planet, they realized that this world was offering them something even more profound—a new way of being, a new connection to the universe.

As they stood there, bathed in the light of the crystals, they knew that their journey was only just beginning. The transformation they had undergone was not merely physical—it was spiritual. They were becoming something new, something more in tune with the wild, untamed energy of the universe.

And as they began to explore the chamber, their hearts filled with hope and wonder, they knew that the future, though uncertain, was filled with endless possibilities.

The Lyrans had found their new home. And with it, they had found a new purpose.

Chapter 7: The Awakening of Lyana

It was a warm summer evening in 2024, the air heavy with the scent of pine and honeysuckle that drifted through the quiet streets of Lawrenceville, Georgia. The sun was beginning to set, casting a golden glow over the small Southern town. Inside the Hartley household, the atmosphere was thick with anticipation. Lyana sat at the kitchen table, her ice-white hair glimmering in the fading light. Her amber, cat-like eyes watched her parents carefully, waiting for them to say what she had always sensed was coming.

There had always been something different about her, something that set her apart from everyone else. She wasn't just unusual because of her striking appearance—her ebony skin, white hair, pointed ears, and those piercing eyes that made people stare longer than they should—it was something deeper. There was a distance she felt from the world around her, an intangible gap between who she was and the life she had been living.

Her parents, Zyra and Talen Hartley, had always been kind and loving, but she knew they were hiding something from her. She could sense it in the way they hesitated when she asked about her childhood, in the way they deflected questions about their past. And now, after years of subtle avoidance, they had finally decided to tell her the truth.

Zyra cleared her throat, her normally confident voice tinged with nervousness. "Lyana," she began, "there's something we need to tell you. Something we should have told you a long time ago."

Talen, her father, sat beside her, his golden eyes reflecting the weight of the moment. He reached for Zyra's hand, and the two shared a look—one of deep understanding and love, but also of fear. They had protected Lyana for so long, but the time for secrets was over.

"We weren't born here, Lyana," Talen said softly, his voice calm yet serious. "We're not from Earth."

Lyana frowned, her heart pounding in her chest. She had always felt this truth lurking beneath the surface, but hearing it spoken aloud was something entirely different.

Zyra's voice trembled slightly as she continued. "We're from a star system called Lyra. It was our home before we came to Earth. You were born there, Lyana."

Lyana's breath caught in her throat. "I was born there?" she repeated, the words feeling foreign and strange on her tongue. She had always thought of herself as different, but this was beyond anything she could have imagined. "Why didn't you tell me?"

"We wanted to protect you," Talen said gently. "You were just seven years old when we left Lyra. When we arrived on Earth, we made the decision to block your memories of our home. We thought it would be easier for you to live a normal life here, to grow up like a human child. We were waiting for the right time to tell you... but we didn't realize how difficult that would be."

Lyana's head spun. The vague, hazy memories of her early childhood suddenly felt sharper, clearer. Flashes of light, warmth, and peace filled her mind—memories that had always been just out of reach, now rushing back to her all at once. "I... I remember," she whispered, her voice trembling. "I remember Lyra. I remember the light... how beautiful it was."

Her parents exchanged relieved glances as her memories slowly began to unlock. Zyra smiled softly, her eyes filled with the same gentle sadness Lyana had always sensed behind her mother's strong exterior. "Yes," Zyra said. "Lyra was beautiful—clean, peaceful, everything in perfect harmony."

The words unlocked more memories, and suddenly Lyana could see it all: the shimmering cities made of crystal, the soft glow of the twin suns that bathed the planet in golden light, the clear air that smelled of flowers and fresh rain. She could remember running through wide, open fields as a child, feeling the warmth of Lyra's suns on her skin. She had felt so free there, so alive in ways she hadn't understood as a child but now recognized as a deep connection to the very essence of her home world.

"I remember," she repeated, her eyes filling with tears. "It was perfect. Why did we leave?"

Talen's face darkened. "Our world was destroyed, Lyana. The Dracos, a powerful and ruthless race, invaded our star system. They wanted the energy of our crystals, the power that fueled Lyra. They destroyed everything in their path, and we had no choice but to flee. We escaped to Earth, along with a few others, but our home is gone now."

The weight of her father's words pressed down on Lyana, the sense of loss cutting through her like a blade. The memories of Lyra that had once felt warm and distant now filled her with a deep ache. To know that her childhood home, with its serenity and beauty, had been obliterated—it was almost too much to bear.

Her mother's hand rested gently on hers, grounding her in the moment. "We wanted you to have a life here on Earth, to grow up without the fear and pain of losing your home," Zyra explained. "But we knew that one day, you would need to know the truth. You've always been different, Lyana, and now you understand why."

Lyana nodded, her mind racing as she tried to process everything. Her memories of Earth were nothing like her memories of Lyra. Earth felt chaotic, loud, and polluted. The humans around her were driven by ambitions and fears that she had never quite understood. She had always felt out of place, even though she had learned to fit in. Now, she realized it was because her very being was tied to a different world—a world she had lost.

"And my memories? Why did you block them?" Lyana asked, her voice softer now, more vulnerable. "Was it really to protect me?"

Talen sighed deeply, his eyes filled with regret. "We thought it would make things easier for you. You were so young, and we didn't want you to live with the pain of losing Lyra. But in doing that, we also took away your sense of who you really are. That was our mistake, and we're sorry."

Zyra added, "You're Lyran, Lyana. You always have been, even if you didn't remember it. The things that made you feel different here on Earth—your abilities, your instincts—they come from who you are, from where you came from."

Lyana stared at her parents, her heart full of questions and emotions she didn't know how to express. She had always felt different, yes, but now that difference had a name, a history. She wasn't just an outlier in human society; she was something else entirely. "What does this mean for me now? Am I supposed to... do something?"

Zyra's expression softened. "You've always had a purpose, Lyana, even if it hasn't been clear until now. We came to

Earth for a reason—not just to escape, but to help. The Earth is struggling, and humanity is on the brink of a great transformation. You, as a Lyran, have a role to play in that transformation."

Lyana's mind flashed to her experiences in school. She had always been drawn to environmental science, to sustainable technology, even before she fully understood why. Her acceptance into Georgia Tech to study sustainable engineering suddenly felt like more than just a personal choice—it felt like destiny.

"You're going to discover things about yourself, Lyana," Talen said gently. "Your memories are only just beginning to resurface, and with them will come abilities and instincts that you've long forgotten. But now that you know the truth, you can begin to embrace who you truly are."

The truth was a weight lifted off her shoulders, and yet it came with an entirely new set of responsibilities. Lyana had always excelled in her studies, driven by a desire to make a difference in the world, but now it seemed that her desire was tied to something far deeper. She wasn't just another student trying to find her place in the world—she was part of something ancient, something cosmic.

In the days that followed, the memories of Lyra continued to flood back to her. She remembered more than just the beauty of the star system; she remembered her friends, the games they used to play under the twin suns, the joy of feeling truly at home. She remembered the smooth, crystalline buildings that seemed to hum with energy and life, the way the entire planet felt like it was in perfect balance with the universe.

But she also remembered the fear. She remembered the whispers of the Dracos' approach, the way the adults had begun to act more serious, more secretive. And she remembered the night they had left—the hurried escape, the last glimpse of her home as it was swallowed by darkness.

Georgia Tech became a place of new beginnings, but it was no longer just about academics. For Lyana, it was about understanding who she was and what she was meant to do. She began her coursework in sustainable engineering with a sense of urgency, determined to find solutions for Earth that echoed the harmony and balance she remembered from Lyra.

At times, it was overwhelming. She would sit in her classes, surrounded by other students, and feel the strange disconnect between her past and their present. While her peers talked about exams and internships, Lyana's mind often drifted to the stars, to the life she had lived before Earth. She found herself doodling sketches of Lyra's cities in her notebooks, her mind returning to memories that felt more like dreams.

It wasn't long before she began to question her purpose. If she had been sent to Earth with the knowledge of her people, was she meant to use that knowledge to help humanity? Was that why she was here? And if so, how could she, a single person—alien or not—make a difference on a planet so vast and so troubled?

The answer, it seemed, was buried within her memories, waiting to be unlocked.

As her memories continued to return, Lyana began to sense a deeper connection to the Earth itself. She could feel the energy of the planet in ways she had never been able to before. It was faint, buried beneath the pollution and chaos of human civilization, but it was there—alive and vibrant, waiting to be nurtured.

One evening, as she walked across campus, Lyana paused at the edge of a small wooded area. The trees stood tall and silent, their leaves rustling softly in the evening breeze. She closed her eyes and reached out with her senses, feeling the life within the forest, the subtle hum of energy that pulsed beneath the surface. It reminded her of Lyra, of the way everything had been connected, living in perfect harmony.

But Earth was different. The planet's energy was fractured, strained under the weight of human progress and destruction. It needed healing. And for the first time, Lyana understood that she had the power to help.

Her studies in sustainable engineering began to take on new meaning. She wasn't just learning about renewable energy and conservation—she was reconnecting with her Lyran heritage. The technologies and ideas she developed in class felt familiar, as if she were remembering them rather than learning them for the first time. She could see how they could be improved, how the Earth's energy could be harnessed and balanced in a way that would restore the planet, not deplete it.

But with this knowledge came a growing sense of responsibility. If she had the ability to help Earth, then wasn't it her duty to do so?

One afternoon, as Lyana sat in the library, buried in her work, she felt a presence behind her. Turning, she saw her professor, Dr. Ellis, standing there, a curious expression on his face. "You've been working on something different, haven't you?" he asked, motioning to her notebooks, which were filled with complex designs and diagrams.

Lyana hesitated for a moment before nodding. "Yes. I've been thinking about new ways to harness energy—ways that might be more in tune with the planet's natural rhythms."

Dr. Ellis raised an eyebrow. "That's an ambitious idea. And from what I've seen of your work, you might just be onto something."

Lyana felt a rush of pride and anxiety all at once. She knew she was onto something—something bigger than even her professor could understand. But how could she explain that her ideas weren't just academic? That they came from a place far beyond Earth?

That night, back in her dorm room, Lyana sat by the window, gazing up at the stars. The memories of Lyra were sharper now—clearer than they had ever been. She could remember her life before Earth, before everything had changed. And yet, this planet was now her home. She had to reconcile her two identities: the girl from a small town in Georgia and the Lyran who had once walked among the stars.

The stars twinkled in the sky, distant and cold, but familiar. She wasn't alone in this. Her parents had come here with her, and there were others like them scattered across the planet—other Lyrans who had escaped the destruction of their home. They, too, carried the knowledge of their people, waiting for the right time to reveal themselves, to help guide humanity toward a future in balance with the Earth.

Lyran Legacy: The Starseed Chronicles Begin

Lyana knew that she was a part of something larger than herself. She had a mission, a purpose that was beginning to unfold before her. She wasn't just here to study or to live a quiet, ordinary life. She was here to bring the wisdom of Lyra to Earth, to help heal this planet before it was too late.

And now, with her memories unlocked and her heritage revealed, she knew what she had to do. Her path was clear. She would use her knowledge—both human and Lyran—to create technologies that would restore balance to the Earth. She would combine the best of both worlds to bring harmony to a planet that desperately needed it.

For the first time in her life, Lyana felt truly at peace. She knew who she was. She was Lyran, a child of the stars, and her journey was only just beginning

Chapter 8: Lyra's Call to Action

Lyran Legacy: The Starseed Chronicles Begin

Lyana stared out of the floor-to-ceiling windows of her sleek office, perched on the 80th floor of one of New York's most advanced skyscrapers. The city hummed beneath her, alive with a chaos only humans could create. Horns blared, people rushed from one crisis to another, and the constant push for more — more wealth, more success, more everything — filled the air like static electricity.

She sipped her coffee, a blend she imported from a boutique roaster who swore it was sustainable. That word, "sustainable," made her laugh. If only Earthlings knew what sustainability really looked like. Her thoughts drifted, as they often did, to Lyra. Oh, how breathtaking her world had been before the Draco destroyed it. Shimmering skies filled with hues of purple and gold, the air tinged with a magic that made every breath feel like a connection to the stars themselves.

Here on Earth, the air is thick, clogged with pollution and tension. Lyana's nose crinkled as she watched a garbage truck rumble past her building below. A metaphor, she thought. Earth was becoming its own wastebasket.

Her phone buzzed, jolting her back to the present. She glanced down and smirked. It was Ella, her Earth friend. Ella was the complete opposite of her in nearly every way — bubbly, naive, and blissfully unaware that her closest friend was an extraterrestrial from a planet light years away. Still, there was something endearing about her.

"Got time for lunch?" the text read.

Lyana shook her head, her ice-white hair swaying against her shoulders. Lunch? Sure, why not? Saving Earth could wait for an hour. She typed a quick response: *Be there in 10.*

She turned back to the window, her reflection catching her cat-like eyes and pointed ears — the only physical markers of her true nature. The rest of her appearance was unremarkable by human standards. To Ella and the rest of New York, she was just another driven entrepreneur, running an AI company that promised to revolutionize the way people interacted with technology and the environment.

Her thoughts wandered as she gathered her things. Humanity had potential, that much she knew. That's why the Starseeds from Lyra had taken refuge on Earth after the Draco destroyed their home. They had once believed this planet could be saved, that its people could rise above their greed, their division.

But every day, the evidence seemed to prove otherwise.

"Humans," she muttered to herself, grabbing her coat, "you've got no idea what you're playing with."

As she left the office, her assistant waved goodbye. Jason, a talented coder who, like everyone else in her orbit, had no clue for whom he was really working.

"Have a great lunch, boss!" he chirped, ever the optimist. If only he knew.

The elevator doors slid shut, and Lyana exhaled slowly, the weight of her mission pressing on her. Centuries of watching, guiding, and nudging humanity forward, and for what? Political divisions were growing deeper, environmental collapse loomed like a storm on the horizon, and technology — though progressing — was still far from what Earth needed to become truly sustainable.

Her company was the best shot she had at making a tangible difference. *SustainTech*, as she called it, was a beacon of hope, developing AI systems designed to solve environmental crises, create new renewable energy sources, and, if she played her cards right, wake people up before it was too late. She needed them to see that their destructive ways weren't just threatening their planet — they were threatening the entire galaxy.

But for now, her focus was simpler: *Eat lunch with Ella and pretend to be normal.*

The elevator reached the lobby, and as she stepped out into the busy streets, Lyana blended into the crowd. To any passerby, she was just another ambitious woman in a city full of ambitious people.

But deep inside, she knew that every choice, every innovation she pushed for, was one small step toward recreating what had been lost. Lyra may have been destroyed, but the dream of building a new world — a better world — was alive and well.

As she walked toward the café to meet Ella, Lyana smirked at the irony of it all. She was saving Earth, one patent and one coffee date at a time.

Chapter 9: Lyana in Disguise

Lyana had gotten good at pretending. Earth was chaotic, unpredictable, and full of odd customs she never quite understood, but one thing she had mastered? The art of fitting in.

She sat at her desk, spinning a pen between her fingers as she stared at the holographic blueprint for her latest AI technology. *SustainTech's* latest project, a renewable energy grid capable of self-repairing and adapting to any environmental changes, could potentially revolutionize the way humans consume energy. Yet, none of it felt groundbreaking to her. On Lyra, technology like this was obsolete centuries ago. Here, on Earth, they were just catching up, and she had to temper her impatience.

Her office was a reflection of her dual identity. On the surface, it was a modern CEO's workspace: sleek, minimalist, with just the right amount of quirky personal touches. A framed poster that read *"Think Outside the Box...Then Build a New Box"* hung behind her desk. She had carefully curated a sense of relatability—quirky, creative, human.

If only they knew.

There was a knock on her door. Jason, her assistant, poked his head in. "Lyana, the board meeting's in ten. You ready?"

She smiled, a practiced move that conveyed just enough warmth to appear human but not too much to seem overly enthusiastic. "Born ready, Jason."

As he disappeared down the hallway, she leaned back in her chair, her mind slipping into a flashback—her early days on Earth. Back when "Jason" and "board meetings" were foreign concepts, and the idea of running a tech startup was as ridiculous to her as a Draco telling a joke.

Present Day: The CEO

Now, decades later, she was Lyana Stark, CEO of *SustainTech*, and one of the leading figures in the push for innovative sustainability. She had embraced her human disguise fully, crafting a persona that was sharp, witty, and just eccentric enough to be believable. Her ice-white hair was chalked up to an edgy fashion choice, her pointed ears hidden beneath the waves of it. As for her cat-like eyes, she had simply told people she had "really cool contacts."

Her human identity was practically flawless, though sometimes she still slipped. Like when Ella had once caught her staring at the moon for an uncomfortably long time.

"You, okay?" Ella had asked, nudging her. "You're zoning out."

Lyana had blinked, tearing her gaze from the sky. "Just…thinking. Humans are weird, you know?"

Ella laughed, nodding in agreement. "Ain't that the truth."

Ella had been her friend for years, ever since they'd met at a startup conference where Ella was pitching her own eco-friendly fashion line. The friendship had been easy, perhaps too easy. Ella's good-natured obliviousness had made Lyana's life as a disguised Starseed much more manageable.

As she prepared for the board meeting, Lyana reflected on how far she had come. Fitting in with humans wasn't the challenge it had once been, but convincing them to change? That was another story. Humanity was stubborn, clinging to its old ways even as the planet crumbled beneath their feet. Every day, it became clearer to her that they needed a wake-up call.

Her mission was no longer just about guiding them toward technological innovation. It was about saving them from themselves.

She stood up, smoothing her tailored jacket. As much as she enjoyed the game of pretending, sometimes she wished she could just walk into a room and tell everyone the truth: *"I'm not from here. I'm from a planet you've never heard of. And if you don't start listening, you're going to end up just like it— gone."*

But that wasn't how Earth worked. Humans needed subtlety, nudges in the right direction, gentle pushes disguised as innovation.

For now, Lyana Stark, CEO of *SustainTech*, would do her part, leading humanity toward a brighter, more sustainable future. She would continue blending in, using her sharp wit and creative solutions to inspire innovation. But deep down, she knew this mission was about much more than AI or renewable energy.

It was about waking them up—before it was too late.

Chapter 10: The World is Falling Apart

Lyana sat in her office, staring blankly at the newsfeed scrolling across the wall. The headlines were all the same: political upheaval, environmental disasters, and yet another scandal from one of the world's so-called leaders. Every word screamed chaos.

Her coffee, which once brought her a modicum of comfort, sat cold and forgotten on her desk. Today was one of those days—one of those *heavy* days—when pretending was harder than usual. Earth was unraveling before her eyes, and no matter how many brilliant minds she'd helped shape, no matter how many innovations she'd ushered into existence, it was starting to feel like putting a bandage on a sinking ship.

She exhaled slowly, rubbing her temples, her mind heavy with the weight of everything happening around her. Decades of work, building her company, guiding entrepreneurs toward solutions, all seemed futile when the world itself refused to change.

Systemic problems require systemic solutions.

Her thoughts flickered back to Lyra. On her home planet, there had been a time of crisis, too. But Lyra had something Earth lacked unity. Lyra had faced its challenges as one, a collective effort to preserve the beauty and magic of their world. Earth, on the other hand? Humans couldn't even agree on how to save themselves. They fought over resources, polluted their own skies, and elected leaders who seemed more intent on lining their own pockets than ensuring the survival of their species.

And then there was the innovation problem.

For years, Lyana had poured her energy into mentoring Earth's brightest entrepreneurs. She had scouted talent, attended pitch meetings, and invested in countless startups that promised to revolutionize the world. Some of them had, briefly. A new sustainable fashion line here, a groundbreaking renewable energy tech there—but the problems were bigger than these small wins.

She leaned back in her chair, recalling her past successes. She had personally coached a handful of the planet's most innovative minds, helping them break free of the rigid thinking that held humanity back. There was Ravi, the young Indian engineer who had developed solar panels so efficient they could power entire cities. Or Mei, the environmental scientist who had created a filtration system that could clean the most polluted water sources.

Those were the days when she still believed in individuals. When she thought that guiding the right people would lead to a ripple effect—a wave of change that would spread through humanity.

But now? Now, the problem seemed so much larger than any one person could fix.

Lyana's frustration simmered beneath the surface. The truth was painfully clear: it wasn't just that some people were refusing to innovate. It was that the systems in place were designed to stifle creativity, to keep humanity in a cycle of dependence on outdated technology and unsustainable practices. Earth was suffocating under its own weight, and its people were too distracted by trivial problems to see it.

She clenched her jaw, staring at the screen as the news anchor reported yet another record-high inflation rate. Humans couldn't even manage their resources properly, let alone fix their planet.

The memory of Lyra's destruction hit her like a wave. She closed her eyes and let it wash over her, seeing it in vivid flashes: the Draco ships appearing out of nowhere, the sky turning a deep, unnatural red, the panic that swept through her people as they realized they had been betrayed by the very forces they had once trusted. Lyra had been a paradise, and they had watched it burn because they had failed to act in time.

Now, Earth was following the same path, and it was happening right in front of her eyes. The parallels were haunting.

The Systemic Problem

Lyana's thoughts drifted to the last conference she attended—an exclusive summit for world leaders and top innovators. She had sat through hours of panels, listening to speeches that were full of empty promises and half-baked solutions. It was all about money, power, and ego. Every decision was motivated by short-term gain, with no regard for the long-term consequences. It was maddening.

She had watched as they patted themselves on the back for incremental changes, for slightly improving technologies that should have been leaps ahead by now.

"Incremental doesn't work when your house is on fire," she had muttered under her breath during one of the sessions, earning a confused look from the man sitting next to her.

The problem wasn't the innovators themselves, at least not entirely. Many of them had the potential to bring real change. But the structures surrounding them—the governments, the corporations, the global powers that controlled resources— were the ones holding humanity back. Lyana could see it all so clearly, but whenever she tried to push things forward, she hit the same walls.

Humans were on the verge of losing something precious. Their spirit of innovation, that creative spark that had brought them out of the Stone Age and into the world of technology, was fading. Not because they weren't capable, but because they were being stifled by the very systems they had built.

Reflections on the Bigger Problem

She leaned forward, propping her chin on her hand. Humans were always proud of their past achievements. The Industrial Revolution, the Space Race, the birth of the Internet—these were the milestones they clung to, as if resting on those laurels was enough. But Lyana knew better. The real challenge wasn't in what they had done—it was in what they were failing to do now.

Humanity had stopped dreaming big. They had become too comfortable, too complacent. Their societies were designed to keep things running smoothly, not to encourage radical, world-changing ideas. And that, she realized, was the heart of the problem. If they couldn't break free of that mindset, Earth was doomed to follow in Lyra's tragic footsteps.

She stood up from her desk, pacing the length of her office. There had to be a way to change the system from the inside. It wasn't enough to inspire individuals anymore. The entire structure needed to be overhauled. But how? She was only one Starseed, operating in disguise as a tech entrepreneur. Could she really change the course of an entire planet?

Lyana stopped at the window, looking out over the city. The sun was setting, casting a golden hue over the skyscrapers.

She watched as people bustled below, living their lives, oblivious to the impending collapse they were hurtling toward.

Sometimes, she wondered if humanity even wanted to be saved. They had all the tools, all the intelligence, and yet they chose to remain stuck in destructive patterns. Was it fear? Or simply a lack of vision? She wasn't sure anymore.

The Last Straw

The thought of giving up crossed her mind for the first time in years. Maybe Earth wasn't worth saving. Maybe it was destined to fall apart, just like Lyra. But then, as if on cue, her phone buzzed with a notification.

It was a message from Ella.

"Hey, just saw your latest project in the news! Incredible stuff. You're going to change the world, girl."

Lyana chuckled to herself. Ella had no idea how literal that statement was.

Still, her friend's enthusiasm reignited something in her. Maybe Ella was right. Maybe there was still hope.

Perhaps the answer wasn't to change humanity, but to guide it toward rediscovering its lost spirit of innovation. Maybe, just maybe, Lyana could help them dream big again.

With renewed determination, she turned away from the window, a plan forming in her mind. She would tackle the problem from all angles—systemic change, technological revolution, and a new way of thinking. It wasn't too late. Not yet.

Chapter 11: A Signal From The Stars

Lyana sat at her desk, tapping her fingers absently on the surface as her eyes scanned the latest reports on *SustainTech's* progress. Renewable energy grids were slowly being implemented in key cities, and their AI solutions for sustainable living had been well-received by early adopters. But the larger issues remained. Earth's problems weren't just technological—they were deeply embedded in the systems of power, and she knew that no amount of innovative tech alone could fix that.

Suddenly, a soft hum filled the room. Her eyes flicked toward the source of the sound, her heart racing in a way it hadn't in centuries. The sound was unmistakable, and it wasn't coming from any Earth-made device.

It was coming from Lyra.

Lyana quickly turned off the monitors and closed the door to her office, ensuring no one could interrupt. She took a deep breath, steeling herself. It had been centuries since she'd heard anything from her home. Lyra was gone, destroyed by the Draco. But the Starseeds who had escaped were scattered across the galaxy, many of them right here on Earth, hidden just as she was. The signal she was hearing now was a call—something she had feared but also hoped for.

Her hands trembled as she activated the small, round device hidden in the corner of her office, a relic from Lyra that had remained dormant for so long. The device hummed to life, casting a soft glow around the room. It was a communication beacon, something the Starseeds had used to stay in touch across vast distances. Now it was picking up a transmission from deep within the galaxy.

"Lyana Stark," a calm, familiar voice said, as the beacon projected a shimmering hologram of a figure she recognized

immediately. It was Zoran, one of the leaders of the Starseed Council, a group of the most revered elders from Lyra.

For a moment, Lyana could barely breathe. The sight of Zoran—an elder Starseed she hadn't seen since the fall of Lyra—made her chest tighten with emotion. His face was lined with age and wisdom, his ice-blue eyes glinting with the same intensity she remembered from long ago.

"Zoran," she whispered, her voice barely audible. *"I didn't think there were any of us left who could still communicate..."*

"There are more of us than you know," Zoran replied, his holographic image flickering slightly. *"And now we need to gather. Earth is reaching its tipping point. The Starseeds cannot remain in hiding any longer."*

Lyana's mind raced. She had known this moment would come eventually, but she had hoped there would be more time— more time to help Earth turn things around without resorting to the full force of the Starseeds.

"What are you asking me to do?" Lyana asked, already knowing the answer.

"It's time for the Starseeds on Earth to unite. We need to pool our knowledge, our resources, and our abilities if we are to reverse the decline you've been witnessing. The chaos is spreading faster than anticipated. Humanity's creative spirit is faltering, and without intervention, their chance at survival will vanish."

Lyana felt a deep weight settle in her chest. She had spent centuries hiding her true nature, blending in, working from the shadows to inspire innovation and guide humanity. But she had always done it alone, believing that subtlety was the best way to protect the planet. Now, it seemed that subtlety would no longer suffice.

"How many of us are there?" she asked, her voice tight.

"More than you realize," Zoran said, his tone steady. *"We've been watching, just as you have. Some have been in key positions, quietly influencing leaders and thinkers. Others have chosen more isolated paths, working with the planet itself, protecting what remains of its natural resources. But we are scattered and disconnected. If we unite, our collective power could change the course of this world."*

Lyana's mind whirred with possibilities. The Starseeds were more powerful than humans could ever comprehend. Each of them carried with them the wisdom and technology of Lyra, abilities far beyond anything Earth had ever seen. If they united, they could indeed change everything. But doing so would also mean revealing themselves—a risk that could have unforeseen consequences.

"Gathering the Starseeds will be dangerous," she said cautiously. *"If we're discovered, humanity may not react well. They're...not ready."*

Zoran nodded. *"I understand your concerns. But Earth's situation grows more dire by the day. This world is on the brink of environmental and societal collapse. If we don't act now, it will be too late. We cannot afford to wait any longer for humanity to come to its senses on its own."*

Lyana's heart sank as she realized the truth in his words. Earth had been given every chance to correct its path, but it seemed determined to spiral into chaos. The political divisions, the environmental destruction, the greed, and corruption—it was all leading toward an inevitable collapse.

If the Starseeds were going to act, it had to be now.

"What's the plan?" she asked, her voice filled with the steely resolve of someone ready for a fight.

"First, you must locate the other Starseeds," Zoran said. *"Many of them have gone into deep cover, and their identities are not known even to us. But you, Lyana—you have a way of finding people. Use your connections, your influence. Bring them together. Once we are united, we can begin the work of rebuilding."*

Lyana nodded. It was a monumental task, but if anyone could do it, it was her. She had built an empire from the ground up on Earth, and she had learned how to navigate human society better than most. If the Starseeds were scattered, she would find them. She would bring them together, and they would make humanity remember what it was like to dream again.

Zoran's hologram flickered once more, his face softening. *"You've done well, Lyana. You've given this world more hope than you know. But now, it's time to go beyond hope. It's time for action."*

Before she could respond, the signal faded, leaving the room in silence once more. Lyana stood still, the weight of the moment pressing down on her. She had known this day would come, but now that it was here, it felt overwhelming.

More Starseeds, she thought, letting the idea settle into her mind. She wasn't alone. There were others, like her, who had been quietly working among the humans, guiding them, helping them. But they were isolated, disconnected from each other. That was about to change.

Lyana moved to the window, staring out at the city below. The sun had set, casting the skyline in a dark, shadowy glow. The world was falling apart, but there was still time. With the Starseeds united, they could reshape Earth, guide humanity back to the path of innovation and cooperation. But it wouldn't be easy.

She knew that gathering the Starseeds would change everything. It would mean revealing their true nature, risking exposure, and possibly drawing the attention of forces beyond Earth's borders. There were other beings in the universe—dangerous ones—who would not take kindly to a resurgence of Starseed power.

But that didn't matter now. Lyana had a mission, and she wasn't about to let fear stop her.

Taking a deep breath, she turned back to her desk, her mind already running through the list of potential allies she had met over the years. Some of them had seemed...different. Like they were hiding something, just as she was. She had suspected they might be Starseeds, but she hadn't pursued it. Now, she would.

Time to find my people, she thought, her resolve hardening.

The signal from the stars had been clear. The Starseeds were needed. And Lyana was ready to lead them.

Chapter 12: Reuniting with Old Friends

The hum of Lyana's car—a sleek, electric vehicle she'd customized far beyond Earth's current technology— whispered through the open road as she sped toward the first stop on her cross-country quest: Max.

Max. The name alone made her chuckle. Of all the Starseeds scattered across Earth, he had to be the one she tracked down first. Years ago, he had been one of the brightest minds in sustainable energy, a prodigy of innovation with the power to manipulate energy flows on a molecular level. If anyone could help her kickstart a revolution in human innovation, it was Max. But the problem wasn't his ability. It was his attitude.

Max had grown disillusioned with humanity long before most Starseeds had even settled into their human disguises. He had thrown himself into Earth's energy crises, creating renewable solutions that had the potential to power entire nations. But after decades of watching his breakthroughs get tangled in bureaucratic red tape, corrupted by corporate greed, or simply ignored by people too short-sighted to embrace real change, Max had become, in his own words, "too old and too tired to care."

Lyana wasn't going to let him wallow in cynicism any longer.

The road stretched ahead of her, wide and empty, as she cruised through the Midwest. Fields of wind turbines flanked the highway, spinning lazily in the breeze. They were a pale imitation of the energy harnessing systems she had seen on Lyra. Earth had so much potential, but it was always limited by its own self-inflicted wounds.

She tapped the console, opening a map that showed the location of Max's hideout—a tiny, unassuming cabin in the middle of nowhere, surrounded by nothing but farmland and more turbines. Max had gone full recluse after his last project was shut down. He didn't answer calls, he didn't attend conferences anymore, and according to one source, he had a collection of very angry letters to the editor in various scientific journals. All signs pointed to a man who had given up.

Perfect.

As she neared the location, the car's AI system chimed. "Approaching destination. Max's cynicism was detected at 98%. Prepare for sarcasm."

Lyana snorted. ***"Prepare for sarcasm,"*** indeed. She pulled the car off the main road and into a gravel driveway that led to the small cabin, nestled between two towering wind turbines. A single light was on inside, casting a warm glow against the backdrop of the darkening sky. She parked the car, took a deep breath, and braced herself for what was sure to be a challenge.

She knocked on the door, and after a long pause, it creaked open just enough for her to see one hazel eye glaring at her from the crack. Max.

"Lyana," he said flatly, his voice dripping with boredom. "If you're here to pitch me another world-saving idea, you might want to turn around now. I'm out of the world-saving business."

Lyana flashed him her most charming grin. "Good thing I'm not here to *pitch* anything. I'm here to drag you out of your self-imposed misery and get you back into action. You know, the fun stuff."

Max's eye narrowed. "Fun? You must be lost. There's no fun here. Only the sound of turbines spinning and the sweet, sweet hum of inevitable planetary collapse."

She pushed the door open a little more, forcing her way inside with the same stubbornness she had employed for centuries. "Come on, Max. You can't fool me. You still care. You're just pretending not to."

Inside, the cabin was as unremarkable as she'd expected bookshelves crammed with scientific journals, a couch buried under what looked like months of discarded papers, and several empty coffee mugs scattered across various surfaces. Max, meanwhile, stood with his arms crossed, his hair slightly longer than the last time she'd seen him, his face set in a scowl that couldn't quite hide the spark of curiosity in his eyes.

"Still playing the role of the eternal optimist, I see," he muttered, slumping into a chair, and rubbing his temples. "Let me guess—you've come to tell me how we're all going to unite and save Earth from itself, and I'm supposed to drop everything and join your merry band of hopefuls."

"Pretty much," Lyana replied, plopping down across from him, and kicking her feet up on a nearby ottoman. "Except this time, it's not just about saving Earth. It's about waking humanity up. And I could really use your help."

Max rolled his eyes. "Waking them up? Have you seen what's happening out there? They're more interested in social media influencers and conspiracy theories than in real solutions. No one wants to change. Not really. I spent decades giving them the keys to a sustainable future, and all I got in return was rejection and disappointment."

Lyana leaned forward; her tone playful but pointed. "Come on, Max. You're not fooling anyone. You loved that work, and you know it. Sure, the bureaucrats are useless, and the corporations are corrupt, but you weren't doing it for *them*.

You were doing it because you believed in it. And you still do. Otherwise, you wouldn't be out here, hiding in this cozy little apocalypse bunker."

He groaned, running a hand through his messy hair. "I'm not hiding. I'm—" He paused, searching for a better word. "—retired."

Lyana laughed. "Please. You're about as retired as I am. You just got tired of beating your head against the wall. But that's why I'm here. I'm not asking you to keep doing the same thing. I'm asking you to join me, and a whole bunch of others like us, in something bigger."

Max raised an eyebrow, though his cynicism remained firmly in place. "Others? You mean the other Starseeds? Let me guess—they're all still out there, pretending to be human, hoping that one day humanity will pull its head out of its...well, you know."

"Not hoping," she corrected. "Acting. We've been watching, working in the background, but now it's time to do something more direct. And that's where you come in."

Max sighed, leaning back in his chair. "Why me? There are other Starseeds with energy manipulation skills. I'm not special."

"Because you're the best," she said simply, folding her arms. "And you care, even if you pretend not to. Plus, if you don't help, I'll be forced to do the whole thing solo, and you know I'll just end up calling you every day to complain about it."

He gave a small, reluctant smile. "That sounds terrible."

"It really would be," she agreed, flashing him a grin. "Besides, I know you miss the challenge. Sitting out here, moping around with your turbines can't be *that* satisfying. I've got something better—something that could actually change things."

Max squinted at her, skeptical but intrigued. "Change things, huh? How? More AI? Another energy grid that'll get swallowed up by corporate nonsense?"

Lyana's smile faded, and she leaned forward, her voice taking on a more serious tone. "No. This time, it's about gathering the Starseeds. All of them. We unite, we pool our talents, and we use our abilities in ways humanity hasn't seen before. We've stayed hidden for too long. If we want to help this planet, we can't keep playing by the rules they set. We need to remind them what innovation really looks like."

For a long moment, Max said nothing. His eyes flicked toward the window, where the wind turbines turned lazily in the evening breeze. He rubbed his chin, clearly torn between his frustration with humanity and the undeniable pull of his old passion for problem-solving.

Finally, he sighed. "Alright, Stark. You've got my attention. But if I'm going to do this, we do it my way. No boardrooms, no bureaucrats, and definitely no more of those *stupid* TED Talks."

Lyana grinned, extending her hand. "Deal. Welcome back to the world of the living, Max."

He hesitated for a moment, then shook her hand. "Just remember, when this all goes south and humans prove they're not worth the effort, I reserve the right to say, 'I told you so.'"

Lyana laughed, standing up and grabbing her coat. "Fair enough. Now, pack your bags. We've got more Starseeds to find, and I'm not doing this road trip alone."

Max groaned, but there was a light in his eyes that hadn't been there before. "Road trip? This better not involve bad motel coffee."

"Depends on your definition of bad," she teased, heading toward the door. "But hey, I'll make sure to bring snacks."

As the two of them walked out of the cabin and into the twilight, Lyana felt the familiar thrill of adventure bubbling up inside her. She had convinced Max—one of the most cynical Starseeds on the planet—to join her cause. And if she could get him on board, the rest of them didn't stand a chance.

Chapter 13: A Starseed In Politics

Lyana parked her car outside the towering marble building, staring up at the façade with a mix of amusement and dread. Washington, D.C. always had a way of making her feel like she was walking into a chess game where all the pieces were rigged. Politics was a world she had mostly avoided during her time on Earth—too messy, too complicated, too full of people who thrived on saying a lot without really saying anything at all.

But today, she wasn't here to debate policy or meet with some human bureaucrat. She was here to find Zora.

Zora was, by far, one of the most talented Starseeds Lyana had ever known. Sharp, quick on her feet, and a master of strategy, Zora had embedded herself into the world of politics not long after arriving on Earth. She had risen to prominence as a political strategist, shaping campaigns and policies behind the scenes, quietly steering human decision-making. If anyone understood how power truly worked on this planet, it was Zora. But recently, Lyana had heard whispers that her old friend was burned out—jaded from years of trying to reform a system that seemed hopelessly entrenched in its own corruption.

Lyana wasn't going to let Zora slip away into disillusionment. She needed her on this mission. Zora's understanding of human politics—and her wit—were going to be crucial if they were going to inspire the kind of entrepreneurial revolution humanity so desperately needed.

The revolving doors spun Lyana into the heart of the bustling lobby, filled with polished marble, shiny brass, and the faint whiff of ego. She scanned the room until her eyes landed on a familiar face—Zora, standing by a large window, phone pressed to her ear, waving her free hand in the air with all the

126

exasperation of someone who had just lost her last ounce of patience.

Lyana made her way over, catching snippets of Zora's conversation. It didn't take long to figure out that Zora was verbally tearing into some poor intern who had likely bungled an important campaign strategy.

"I don't care if it's 3 a.m.," Zora said, her tone clipped. "If the senator wants to win, we don't lose momentum. Tell him to stop tweeting and start shaking hands—*in person*. Humans still like a little face-to-face time, last I checked."

She hung up and turned around just as Lyana approached, a look of surprise flashing across her face before it quickly shifted to a smirk.

"Well, well," Zora said, crossing her arms. "Look who decided to pay me a visit. What's the matter, Lyana? You run out of renewable energy grids to save the world?"

Lyana grinned, leaning against the window beside her. "Actually, I'm expanding my horizons. And I need your help."

Zora raised an eyebrow. "You're joking, right? You know I'm done with this whole 'saving the world' gig. Burned that bridge years ago. I'm just trying to keep the ship from sinking too fast now."

Lyana shook her head. "You're not fooling me, Zora. I know you still care. And I know you're bored out of your mind trying to fix this mess from within the system."

Zora sighed dramatically, but her eyes sparkled with the same fire Lyana remembered from their early days on Earth. "Bored" isn't the word. Disillusioned, exhausted, completely over it— that's more accurate."

She led Lyana to a nearby café tucked away in the corner of the building, where the two of them grabbed a table. Zora ordered an espresso, and Lyana opted for tea, settling in as they caught up on the whirlwind of Earth's political theater.

"So," Zora began, her usual dry wit already on display, "let me guess—you want me to jump ship, join your little band of hopefuls, and help fix what humans broke. Again. Sounds like a party."

"Something like that," Lyana replied, smirking. "But I'm not asking you to dive back into the system. This time, we're bypassing the system altogether."

Zora raised an eyebrow, clearly intrigued. "Bypassing the system? You've got my attention. Explain."

Lyana leaned forward, lowering her voice slightly. "You've seen what's happening. The world's falling apart—politically, socially, environmentally. But the root of it all? Humans have lost their entrepreneurial spirit. They're stuck in cycles of fear, division, and greed. They've stopped dreaming, stopped creating. We need to reignite that spark, and I can't do it alone. I'm gathering the Starseeds. It's time for us to unite and push humanity in the right direction—starting with innovation."

Zora sipped her espresso, her eyes narrowing thoughtfully. "And what makes you think humans are even capable of waking up? Most of the ones I've worked with seem pretty content to keep stumbling over the same problems."

Lyana laughed. "Come on, Zora. You've been here long enough to know better. Humans are frustrating, yes. But they're also resilient. They're just... lost right now. They need a push. Something bigger than themselves to believe in. You've been working within this broken political machine long enough to see that, haven't you?"

Zora leaned back in her chair, crossing her arms as she considered Lyana's words. "Yeah, I've seen it. I've watched them trip over themselves time and time again, but every now and then, there's this glimmer—this moment where you think maybe, just maybe, they're on the verge of something great."

Lyana nodded, her tone softening. "Exactly. And we can help them reach that point. But we have to be smart about it. We can't just keep nudging them from behind the scenes. We need to step up. Show them what real innovation looks like. And you? You're the best strategist I know. If anyone can help me figure out how to reignite that entrepreneurial spirit, it's you."

Zora stared at her for a long moment, the weight of Lyana's words settling in. She took another sip of her espresso, letting the silence hang between them. Finally, she spoke, her voice tinged with a mix of sarcasm and sincerity.

"You really know how to make a girl feel special, don't you?" she quipped, though there was a faint smile on her lips.

Lyana grinned. "It's one of my many talents."

Zora let out a long, exaggerated sigh, placing her cup down on the table. "Fine. I'll help. But let's be clear—I'm not diving back into politics. I'm not holding anyone's hand through another PR nightmare. If I'm doing this, it's because I actually believe we can make a difference. And I need to see something *real* come out of it."

Lyana nodded, her grin widening. "Deal. We'll work together, outside the system, and focus on what matters—getting humans to dream again, to create, to solve their own problems."

Zora smirked, leaning closer. "And when this all blows up in your face, just remember—I told you so."

Lyana laughed, shaking her head. "I've already got Max claiming dibs on the 'I told you so' line. You'll have to share it."

Zora's smile broadened, the familiar gleam of mischief in her eyes. "Figures. That grumpy old cynic was always a step ahead. Fine. I'll settle for saying 'I warned you.'"

The two of them laughed together, the tension that had been building for years easing into something lighter, something hopeful. For the first time in a long time, Zora felt like she wasn't just spinning her wheels. Maybe, just maybe, this was a chance to make a real impact.

Lyana stood up, tossing some cash onto the table. "Come on. We've got work to do. I hope you packed your sarcasm, because we've got a road trip ahead of us."

Zora raised an eyebrow. "A road trip? Oh, this is getting better by the minute. Do I at least get to complain the whole way?"

Lyana laughed. "Absolutely. But don't worry—I've got snacks."

As the two Starseeds walked out of the café and into the bustling streets of D.C., Lyana couldn't help but feel a spark of optimism. With Zora on board, their team was growing stronger. And maybe, just maybe, this time they could truly make a difference.

Chapter 14: The Rebel Starseed

Lyran Legacy: The Starseed Chronicles Begin

Lyana sighed as she glanced down at the crumpled piece of paper in her hand. Kai's last known location wasn't exactly what she had hoped for—an abandoned warehouse in the industrial outskirts of Detroit, tucked behind a graffiti-covered alleyway. Of all the Starseeds she needed to find, Kai was the one she was both excited and nervous to confront.

Kai thrived on chaos. His entire existence seemed to orbit around disruption, innovation, and doing whatever he could to break apart the status quo. He was brilliant—there was no question about that—but his methods? Let's just say Kai wasn't exactly the type to play by the rules.

If Zora was all about strategy and Max was the grumpy cynic, Kai was the wild card—unpredictable, full of energy, and constantly teetering between genius and disaster. The last time she'd spoken to him, he had been working on a technology that could potentially destabilize several large corporations overnight, sending the global economy into chaos. She wasn't sure if he'd ever finished that project, but if anyone were capable of bringing down the system with a smirk and a bad joke, it was Kai.

As Lyana parked her car outside the dilapidated warehouse, she couldn't help but smirk. This was *so* Kai. He always did love lurking on the fringes of society, watching as the world's power structures wobbled on the brink of collapse. She took a deep breath and pushed open the car door, stepping out into the crisp, slightly polluted air of Detroit.

The warehouse loomed ahead; its rusted exterior tagged with colorful graffiti. She walked toward the entrance, spotting a small, flickering neon sign hanging above a metal door. It read: *KAI'S CREATIONS: WHERE CHAOS IS KING.*

"Of course," Lyana muttered under her breath, shaking her head with a laugh. She reached for the door and gave it a firm knock.

Nothing.

She knocked again, louder this time. Still nothing. Finally, after a long, awkward pause, the door creaked open just a crack, and a voice called out from inside.

"Password!" the voice said, muffled but unmistakably familiar.

Lyana rolled her eyes. "Kai, it's me. I'm not playing games."

The door swung open, revealing Kai standing in the doorway with his arms crossed, wearing a grease-stained T-shirt, aviator goggles pushed up onto his forehead, and a wide grin plastered across his face.

"Well, well, if it isn't the Queen of Seriousness herself!" Kai exclaimed, throwing his arms wide. "What brings you to my humble abode? Finally ready to join the revolution?"

Lyana stepped inside, looking around the warehouse, which was filled with half-built machines, tangled wires, and piles of old computer parts. Sparks flew from one corner where a small robot was busy welding something. It was as chaotic as she'd imagined—and somehow, it worked.

Kai gestured dramatically to the mess. "Beautiful, isn't it? A little bit of madness goes a long way."

Lyana raised an eyebrow, her arms crossed. "Madness is one word for it. How are you not electrocuted on a daily basis?"

"Luck," he replied with a wink, plopping down onto a nearby couch that looked like it had been fished out of a dumpster. "And a natural talent for avoiding disaster. But hey, I didn't invent that robot dog that accidentally set a conference on fire last year, so I'd say I'm doing better than some of the 'professionals' in my field."

Lyana snorted. "Right. Well, as much fun as it is to watch you create chaos, I'm here on business. I need your help."

Kai leaned back, folding his hands behind his head. "Help, huh? You must be desperate. What's the mission? Smuggling AI chips across borders? Hacking into a billionaire's secret vault? Breaking into Area 51 for some top-secret alien tech?"

"None of the above," Lyana replied, smirking. "Although I'm sure those would all be on your to-do list. No, this time, we're organizing the Starseeds."

Kai sat up straight, his playful grin shifting to one of genuine interest. "Wait. You're serious?"

"As serious as I can be," Lyana said. "I've already recruited Max and Zora. We're going to unite the Starseeds and push humanity toward real innovation, real change. The world's on the brink of collapse, and you know it. We can't stay in the shadows anymore. We need to take action."

Kai stood up, pacing around the warehouse as he chewed on the idea. "Max and Zora, huh? Interesting combo. I'm guessing Max was grumpy about it, and Zora probably made some snarky comments about how hopeless humans are."

"More or less," Lyana said with a chuckle. "But they're on board. And I need you too, Kai. Your ability to disrupt, to create the unexpected—that's what this team is missing. But we need to be organized. This can't just be chaos for chaos's sake."

Kai stopped pacing and turned to face her, his expression suddenly serious. "Look, Lyana. You know I love a good rebellion. And yes, humanity is in a downward spiral. But I don't think they *want* to be saved. Not really. Most people are happy to sit back and watch the world burn as long as they've got their Netflix and cheap fast food."

Lyana shook her head. "I've heard that argument from Max. But I don't buy it. People *do* want to change. They're just stuck. They need a push. And that's where we come in."

Kai studied her for a moment, then let out a long, exaggerated sigh. "Okay, okay. You're right. Humanity needs a kick in the pants. And if anyone can deliver that kick, it's me."

He shot her a mischievous grin, his eyes lighting up with excitement. "But I'm not doing it your way. Oh no. If I'm joining this little crusade, we're doing it with style. Big, loud, disruptive style."

Lyana crossed her arms, smirking. "I expected nothing less. But we do need some structure, Kai. This isn't just about creating chaos. It's about creating *lasting* change."

Kai waved his hand dismissively. "Yeah, yeah, structure, whatever. Just let me do my thing, and we'll have half the corporations on this planet scrambling to keep up. I've got some new tech I've been working on that'll blow their minds—figuratively, of course. Mostly."

Lyana rolled her eyes. "Mostly?"

Kai shrugged. "Eh, details. We'll work out the kinks later."

She couldn't help but laugh. "You really haven't changed, have you?"

"Nope," he replied proudly. "Still the same lovable rebel you've always known."

Lyana moved toward the door, motioning for him to follow. "Alright, come on. We've got more Starseeds to find, and I need someone to keep things interesting along the way."

Kai grabbed a tattered jacket from the back of a chair and slung it over his shoulder. "Interesting? Oh, I'll make things *very* interesting."

As they walked out into the fading light of day, Lyana glanced sideways at Kai. "You know, I've missed this. It's been too long."

Kai grinned. "Same. Let's go make some noise."

Chapter 15: The Entrepreneurial Shift

Lyran Legacy: The Starseed Chronicles Begin

Lyana stood at the podium, the bright lights of the conference hall beaming down on her as she adjusted the mic. Hundreds of eyes watched her with a mix of curiosity and skepticism, waiting for her to speak. This was the fifth *Global Summit for Sustainability and Innovation* she had headlined in a month, and while the audience was packed with top business leaders, influencers, and government officials, she knew that convincing them to change their ways would be a monumental task.

Still, this was why the Starseeds had regrouped—to shift humanity's direction, even if it meant pulling them out of the quicksand of greed and corruption kicking and screaming. And if anyone could inspire that shift, it was Lyana, especially with the team she had behind her.

Taking a deep breath, she plastered on her trademark grin, one part charm and two parts sarcasm. "Well, folks, I hope you've all had your coffee because today, we're going to talk about something more invigorating than your morning espresso—*saving the world* through entrepreneurship." She paused for effect, raising her eyebrows. "No pressure, right?"

The audience chuckled softly, and she continued. "Now, I know what you're thinking: 'Why should I, a billionaire tech CEO or a government official in a suit that costs more than a small car, care about *real* sustainability?' And that's a valid question. I mean, what's a little more pollution, a few more floods, a couple more political crises, am I right?"

The laughter was louder this time, but there was a nervous undertone. Lyana knew how to strike that balance—using humor to ease them in before hitting them with the uncomfortable truth.

She clicked to the next slide on the screen behind her, showing a graphic of a crumbling Earth wrapped in dollar signs. "The reality is, we're running out of time. And the problems we're facing—climate change, resource depletion, political instability—aren't just 'issues for the future.' They're *now* problems. And the only way we're going to fix them is by embracing innovation, entrepreneurship, and sustainability. Not as buzzwords, but as fundamental principles of how we do business."

Her gaze swept across the room. "And that means we have to get creative. We need to think outside the box and, in some cases, set that box on fire."

The audience stirred, some smiling at the image, others clearly more uncomfortable with the idea of burning anything, even metaphorically. But Lyana wasn't here to make them comfortable. She was here to wake them up.

The Global Movement Begins

After the presentation, Lyana stepped down from the stage and was immediately surrounded by reporters and business leaders, eager to ask questions. Max, who had begrudgingly agreed to attend the summit with her, stood off to the side, sipping coffee with an air of mild disinterest.

"How'd I do?" she asked, joining him once the crowd thinned out.

Max shrugged, a small grin tugging at the corner of his mouth. "You certainly know how to keep them entertained. But I doubt half of them are going to change anything once they leave this conference. They'll go back to their boardrooms, make a few token gestures toward sustainability, and then it's business as usual."

Lyana sighed. "I know. That's the problem. We're fighting against a system that thrives on short-term profits. People aren't incentivized to think about the long-term consequences. But we have to start somewhere."

"Somewhere?" Max echoed, raising an eyebrow. "Lyana, we're trying to shift an entire planet's mindset. That's not 'somewhere.' That's *everywhere*."

"Exactly," she replied, her voice filled with a steely determination. "And that's why we're not stopping here. The summits are just the beginning. We're launching the movement."

Max frowned, looking skeptical. "You think a movement's going to be enough to shift the tide against corporate greed and systemic corruption?"

"It's not just about the movement," Lyana explained. "It's about creating the tools for people to break free of the system. We're talking about grassroots entrepreneurship, new models for sustainability, decentralized innovation. We give them the keys, Max. We give them the power to make the change from the ground up."

The Starseeds Unite

Back at *SustainTech's* headquarters, the core team of Starseeds—Lyana, Max, Zora, and Kai—gathered around a table covered with blueprints, diagrams, and plans. It looked like a startup war room, and in many ways, that's exactly what it was. Only this wasn't just about launching a new product. This was about launching a revolution.

"So," Zora said, flicking through a series of reports. "We're aiming to disrupt global systems of power, fuel innovation, and get people to think long-term about sustainability? Piece of cake."

"Don't forget," Kai chimed in, leaning back in his chair with his feet up on the table, "we also need to blow some minds along the way. Make it big, make it loud."

Zora shot him a look. "We're not blowing anything up, Kai."

"Metaphorically speaking," Kai corrected, flashing her a grin. "Mostly."

Max, who had been quietly scanning through some numbers, let out a low whistle. "We've got a lot of work to do. Even if we get the right people on board, the level of corruption we're facing... it's worse than we thought."

Lyana nodded, her face grim. "I know. I've met with the top CEOs, the heads of state, and it's always the same story—talk about change, but as soon as money's on the line, they backtrack. They're stuck in a loop of greed and short-term thinking. And the ones who aren't corrupt are too afraid to step out of line."

Max tossed the report onto the table, his jaw tight. "So, what's our move? If the top is rotten, how do we make sure change happens at the bottom?"

Lyana looked around the room, the faces of her fellow Starseeds—each one powerful, brilliant, and unique. This was her team. And together, they could do what no one else could.

"We create a parallel system," she said, her voice steady. "We give the people tools to innovate, to create their own solutions without relying on corporations or governments. We run workshops, we host seminars, we build platforms that allow entrepreneurs to flourish. It's not about fixing the system from the top down anymore—it's about empowering people from the ground up."

Zora nodded thoughtfully. "So, we sidestep the power structures. We go directly to the people who want change and give them the tools to do it themselves."

"Exactly," Lyana replied. "We'll use the conferences and summits to get the message out, but the real work will be done in the grassroots. We'll train people, we'll invest in new technologies, and we'll connect innovators across the globe."

Kai grinned, his chaotic energy bubbling over. "I love it. It's like an underground tech movement—disrupting everything, leaving no stone unturned. This is going to be fun."

Max, ever the pragmatist, scratched his chin. "But we'll have to be smart. The corporations aren't going to take this lying down. If we start getting traction, they'll try to shut us down. They've got more money and more power than we do."

Lyana smiled; her eyes gleaming with the determination that had driven her for centuries. "Let them try. We're not just some rogue startup. We're Starseeds. And we're about to remind them what real innovation looks like."

Reality Sets In

The next few months were a whirlwind of activity. Lyana and her team hosted workshops, seminars, and training sessions across the globe. They met with aspiring entrepreneurs, grassroots innovators, and local leaders, sharing knowledge, tools, and strategies for sustainable business models. They began to see a shift—a glimmer of hope as people started embracing new ways of thinking.

But it wasn't long before the pushback started.

Corporate interests fought back hard. The first sign came in the form of smear campaigns—anonymous articles questioning the legitimacy of *SustainTech,* and the movement Lyana had sparked. Then came the legal challenges—corporations suing smaller startups that had been inspired by Lyana's message. The system was flexing its muscles, trying to squash the movement before it gained too much momentum.

One evening, after a particularly grueling day of meetings, Lyana sat in her office, exhausted but resolute. Max walked in, his face a mixture of concern and frustration.

"They're not backing down, Lyana," he said, sitting across from her. "The corporations, the politicians—they're doubling down. They see us as a threat."

Lyana rubbed her temples, feeling the weight of it all. "I knew it wasn't going to be easy. But I didn't expect them to move this fast."

Max frowned, leaning forward. "What's the plan? We can't just keep playing defense. If we don't push back, they'll grind us into the ground."

Lyana looked up, her eyes blazing with determination. "We fight back. Harder. We double down on our message. And we remind them that the world is changing—whether they like it or not."

Chapter 16: Corporate Sabotage

Lyran Legacy: The Starseed Chronicles Begin

Lyana had seen many things in her centuries on Earth, but few amused her more than the sheer predictability of corporate greed. Sitting in her office, she read the latest legal threat from one of the world's largest energy conglomerates with a bemused smile.

"*Cease and desist all disruptive activities or face further legal action.* Blah blah blah." She tossed the letter onto the growing pile of similar threats, then spun in her chair to face Max, who was seated across from her, his arms crossed, looking as grumpy as ever.

"They think *this* is going to stop us?" she asked, barely stifling a laugh. "Do they seriously believe we care about their fancy lawyer-speak?"

Max leaned forward, rubbing his temples. "You find this funny, don't you? While I, on the other hand, find this extremely problematic."

"Oh, lighten up, Max. If they're trying this hard, it means we're doing something right," Lyana replied, her grin widening.

Max shook his head, clearly not amused. "They're not just sending letters, Lyana. They're ramping up their attacks. One of our projects in Kenya got shut down last week because of a bogus zoning violation. And Zora's last initiative was tied up in so much bureaucratic red tape, it's practically strangled."

That got Lyana's attention. "Wait—Zora's project is in trouble?"

Max nodded grimly. "That's just the beginning. I've been monitoring communications between some of the big players in energy and politics. They're coordinating now. These guys see us as a legitimate threat, and they're not playing fair anymore."

Lyana leaned back in her chair, her smile fading. For all her humor, she knew Max was right. The system wasn't going to let them change the world without a fight. And now that they were gaining traction, the powers that be—the ones with the most to lose—were starting to push back in ways that went beyond simple intimidation.

Kai burst through the door; his usual chaotic energy dialed up to eleven. "You guys catch the news yet?" he asked, holding up a tablet. "They're coming for us. Full-on smear campaign. I think I saw my face photoshopped onto a cartoon villain's body. It was *not* flattering."

Lyana rolled her eyes. "I'm sure you looked great, Kai. What's the damage?"

He tossed the tablet onto the table, showing a video of a prominent news anchor detailing a "scandal" involving one of their recent projects in South America. The report was full of inaccuracies, twisting their sustainable energy work into a narrative about "foreign influence" and "suspicious tech experiments."

"They're using fear to manipulate the public," Zora said, walking in behind Kai, looking uncharacteristically tired. She tossed her bag on a chair and sat down with a sigh. "This isn't just about stopping us anymore. They're actively trying to turn people against us."

Lyana skimmed through the headlines on Kai's tablet, her brow furrowing. It wasn't just the smear campaign. Their projects were getting shut down, their allies were being targeted, and their movement was being portrayed as dangerous—radical, even. They had expected opposition, but now the attacks were becoming coordinated, ruthless, and increasingly personal.

"Dark forces within corporations and governments," Zora said, echoing what Max had already pointed out. "They're terrified of what we're doing. And they should be. We're taking away their control, their power. And they're going to fight tooth and nail to keep it."

Lyana drummed her fingers on the table, thinking. "So, they've escalated. That just means we need to be smarter about how we move forward."

"Smarter, huh?" Kai quipped, plopping down in a chair. "Well, I suggest we go full 'guerrilla warfare.' Let's sabotage *them* for a change. I've got a few ideas, involving a particularly nasty AI virus I've been working on—"

Zora shot him a warning look. "No. We don't stoop to their level. We play the long game. We outthink them, not out-destroy them."

Kai sighed dramatically but didn't argue. "Fine. Long game it is. But can I at least mess with their social media algorithms?"

"Not yet," Lyana said with a grin. "Let's keep that as a backup plan."

The Threat Becomes Real

It wasn't until later that evening, after the team had scattered to their respective projects, that the severity of the situation hit home for Lyana.

She was back in her office, going through reports when she received a call from one of her closest partners in South America—a woman named Marisol, who had been spearheading a key sustainable water initiative.

"Lyana, we've been raided," Marisol's voice came through, breathless and panicked. "Armed men showed up, claiming to be from the government. They took everything—equipment, data, the works."

Lyana's blood ran cold. "Are you okay? Is anyone hurt?"

"We're okay, but they've shut us down completely," Marisol said, her voice shaking. "They said we're under investigation for... espionage. Lyana, they're framing us."

"I'll take care of it," Lyana promised, already dialing Zora on her other phone. "Stay safe, Marisol. We'll get your project back up and running."

After hanging up, Lyana slumped into her chair. The sabotage wasn't just theoretical anymore. Her allies—good people trying to make real change—were being targeted, intimidated, and shut down. The threat was no longer something she could laugh off with a witty comment and a grin. It was real, and it was dangerous.

Zora answered on the first ring. "I already know," she said, skipping pleasantries. "They're hitting all of our international projects. This is bigger than corporate greed. Governments are in on it, too."

Lyana pinched the bridge of her nose. "What's the strategy? We need to regroup."

Zora was silent for a moment, then she spoke, her voice steady. "We need to play it smart. We go underground with some of our operations, keep things decentralized. If we make ourselves a moving target, they'll have a harder time pinning us down. And we get the public on our side. They can't shut us all down if people start demanding change."

Lyana exhaled, her mind racing. "You're right. We need to inspire a groundswell—something they can't silence with money or threats."

Zora's tone softened. "Look, Lyana, I know you like to keep things light, but this is serious. These people won't hesitate to destroy us if we get too close to threatening their power."

Lyana nodded, feeling the weight of the situation settle over her. "I know. But humor's how I cope, Zora. And besides, we're not done yet."

Regrouping and Strategizing

The following day, Lyana called an emergency meeting with the Starseeds. They gathered in a secluded location, far from prying eyes and ears—an old, renovated barn out in the countryside, where their discussions couldn't be intercepted.

As they sat around the table, the tension was palpable.

"This isn't just about innovation anymore," Max said, his arms crossed tightly. "We're not fighting companies. We're fighting entire power structures that will do anything to maintain control."

"We knew this would happen eventually," Zora said calmly. "We just didn't know how soon they'd retaliate."

Kai leaned back, balancing his chair on two legs. "I say we hit back. Turn their own tech against them. I could have the CEOs of half these companies locked out of their own accounts by morning."

Zora shot him a look. "Or we could not do that."

Lyana stood, commanding everyone's attention. "We're not here to play their game. We're here to change the world, and we can't lose sight of that. Yes, they're pushing back, but that means we're getting closer to the tipping point."

"So, what's the plan?" Max asked, his voice heavy with concern. "How do we fight them without turning this into an all-out war?"

"We go underground," Lyana replied. "We keep innovating, but we do it in a way that's harder to track, harder to target. We keep building the movement from the grassroots up, empowering people to create their own solutions. And most importantly, we get the public on our side. If enough people start demanding change, not even the biggest corporation can stop us."

Kai grinned, clearly enjoying the challenge. "Going underground, huh? Sounds like my kind of party."

Zora looked thoughtful. "We'll need to be smart about this. We can't be too visible, but we can't disappear completely. We'll need to strike the right balance."

Lyana nodded. "Exactly. We're walking a fine line, but if we play this right, we can outsmart them. We've faced worse, and we're still here."

Max gave her a long, serious look. "And what happens when they come after us personally?"

Lyana smiled, but there was steel behind it. "Let them try."

Chapter 17: The Turning Point

Lyana stared at the screen in disbelief, her fingers frozen above the keyboard. She had known they were getting close to something big—too close, apparently—but she hadn't expected *this*. One of her key initiatives, the groundbreaking project in Kenya that promised to revolutionize sustainable energy across the continent, had been completely wiped out.

Everything—years of research, prototypes, funding—gone in the blink of an eye.

"Well, that's fantastic," she muttered to herself, her sarcasm barely masking the anger bubbling beneath the surface. "I always wanted to watch my life's work explode without the courtesy of a fireworks show."

Her phone buzzed, and she glanced at the screen. It was Zora. Of course, Zora already knew. Zora always knew. Lyana let it ring for a few more seconds before picking up, bracing herself for the inevitable bad news dump.

"They took everything," Zora said, skipping pleasantries as usual. "Our lab, our prototypes—it's like they knew exactly where to hit us. This wasn't random sabotage."

Lyana leaned back in her chair, closing her eyes for a moment. "They're not even trying to hide it anymore, are they?"

"Nope. They're playing dirty. Corporate backing, government silence—it's all connected," Zora replied, her voice unusually soft. "They're trying to shut us down completely."

Lyana exhaled, opening her eyes, and staring up at the ceiling. "Well, they're certainly making progress. That project was critical. It wasn't just about energy, Zora. It was the blueprint for all our future initiatives."

"I know," Zora said quietly. "I'll be there in an hour. We need to figure out how to recover from this."

Lyana hung up and stared at her reflection in the dark computer screen. For the first time in years, doubt began creeping in. They had known this battle wasn't going to be easy but watching everything she had worked so hard for unravel in an instant was a blow she hadn't been prepared for.

Maybe Max was right, she thought, the words echoing in her mind. *Maybe humanity doesn't want to be saved. Maybe they're just not ready.*

She stood up, her movements slow and deliberate as she paced the room, trying to shake the heavy weight of frustration and doubt off her shoulders. But the doubts stuck, clinging to her like unwelcome guests.

Her phone buzzed again, this time a message from Kai:

"Hey, Boss Lady, heard about the Kenya thing. Sucks big time. But hey, on the bright side, we've still got all those secret plans hidden away in our 'definitely not a bunker' location, right? We'll be fine. Trust me. Oh, and I found some snacks. Priorities."

Lyana couldn't help but chuckle, despite the situation. Leave it to Kai to bring up snacks in the middle of a crisis. But there was a comfort in that—the chaos he brought always managed to remind her that the world wasn't entirely collapsing. Not yet anyway.

Frustration and Doubt

By the time Zora arrived, Lyana had gone through several stages of emotion—shock, anger, frustration—and had landed somewhere between existential dread and grim determination. Max and Kai were already in the room, Max brooding in the corner while Kai entertained himself by playing with a small drone that buzzed around his head like an overly caffeinated fly.

Zora walked in, her face unreadable as always, and dropped a folder onto the table. "This is everything we've got on the attack. Whoever orchestrated it was thorough."

Max looked up from his brooding. "And well-funded. We're talking top-tier hackers, backed by major players. They wanted this to hurt."

"Well, mission accomplished," Lyana muttered, flipping through the folder. "So, what's our next move? Sit around and hope they don't come for the rest of our projects?"

Kai raised his hand, his drone still zipping around. "I vote for sabotage. Just once. It'll be therapeutic."

Zora shot him a look, but Lyana's lips twitched into a small smile. "Much as I'd love a little payback, we can't afford to lose sight of the goal. We've come too far to let them derail us now."

Max uncrossed his arms, finally speaking up. "They've shown us how serious they are. Now we have to show them how serious *we* are. We need a new plan—something bold, something that gets the public on our side, and fast."

Lyana leaned back in her chair, tapping her fingers on the table as an idea began to take shape. "You're right. We've been playing defense, trying to react to their moves. But what if we flip the script? What if we go public, bigger than we've ever gone before? We don't just push back quietly—we make noise. We tell the world exactly what's happening, and we do it in a way they can't ignore."

Zora looked intrigued. "You're talking about a full-blown message to the world?"

Lyana nodded, the gears in her mind turning faster now. "Yes. A public address—something bold, something viral. We take our message straight to the people. We show them the corruption, the greed, the sabotage. And we call for innovation, for change, for everything we've been working toward."

Kai grinned. "Oh, I like this. Drama, intrigue, a message of hope. You're basically planning a TED Talk on steroids."

Max frowned but nodded. "If we're going to do this, we have to be prepared for them to come after us even harder. They'll try to discredit us, paint us as radicals."

"Let them try," Lyana said, standing up, her confidence returning. "They can't stop all of us. We're not just a few Starseeds playing around with ideas. We're building a global movement, and once we've got the people on our side, no corporation or government will be able to silence us."

Kai clapped his hands together, his excitement bubbling over. "Alright then, let's blow this thing up! Metaphorically, of course. Mostly."

Lyana smiled, her earlier doubts fading. This was the turning point. The moment where they stopped playing by the rules set by the powers that be. They were going to deliver their message to the world, and they were going to do it *their* way.

The Climactic Moment: Delivering the Message

The following week was a blur of planning, strategy sessions, and endless tech troubleshooting, as the Starseeds prepared for their biggest move yet. With Kai's technological expertise,

Zora's strategic mind, and Max's ever-persistent attention to detail, they had orchestrated a plan to broadcast their message to the world.

The day of the broadcast arrived, and Lyana found herself standing on the stage of a small studio that had been transformed into a high-tech command center. Cameras were positioned in every corner, ready to stream their message live to every corner of the planet.

The room buzzed with nervous energy. Zora was on her phone, coordinating last-minute details. Kai was fiddling with a set of holographic displays, while Max stood at the back, arms crossed, his expression grim but determined.

Lyana took a deep breath, stepping in front of the camera. This was it. The culmination of everything they had been fighting for.

The red light on the camera blinked on, and she began.

"Hello, world," she said, her voice steady and strong. "I'm Lyana Stark, CEO of *SustainTech*. But today, I'm speaking to you not as a business leader, but as someone who believes in the power of humanity to innovate, to create, and to change. Over the past few months, our movement has faced opposition from powerful forces—corporations, governments, people who want to maintain control over your future."

She paused, letting the weight of her words sink in. "But we're not here to fight them. We're here to inspire *you*. We believe that the future of this planet doesn't lie in the hands of a few elites, but in the collective power of all of us. Innovation is not a privilege reserved for the few. It belongs to everyone."

Behind her, the holographic displays lit up, showing images of their projects—the ones that had succeeded, the ones that had been sabotaged, and the ones still fighting to survive.

"We've been attacked, sabotaged, discredited. But we're not giving up. And neither should you. This world can change—*you* can change it. Innovation, creativity, entrepreneurship—these are the tools that will build the future. And we're here to help you unlock them."

The message was simple, powerful, and unignorable.

Lyana looked directly into the camera, her voice filled with both humor and conviction. "So, let's stop letting the people who broke this system tell us how to fix it. Let's build something new. Together."

The feed ended, and the room erupted into cheers. Kai pumped his fist in the air, Zora gave a rare smile, and even Max couldn't suppress a small grin.

Lyana stood there, heart pounding, knowing that they had just taken the first real step toward changing the world.

Chapter 18: Humanity's Choice

Lyran Legacy: The Starseed Chronicles Begin

Lyana sat on the rooftop of *SustainTech's* headquarters, gazing out over the city as the setting sun painted the skyline in hues of pink and gold. Below, the streets bustled with the usual hum of urban life, but something felt different. The air seemed charged with new energy, a shift she could almost feel in her bones. It wasn't just the physical world—it was the pulse of something bigger.

For the first time in a long time, people were starting to wake up.

It hadn't been easy. The weeks following their public broadcast had been chaotic. The smear campaigns, the legal challenges, the attempts to discredit them—it all ramped up in a desperate attempt to maintain control. But none of it had worked. The Starseeds' message had struck a chord, resonating with people all over the world.

Small pockets of entrepreneurs, innovators, and dreamers began to emerge—people who had taken up the call, driven by the idea that they could create real change, even in the face of overwhelming opposition. They weren't waiting for governments or corporations to act. They were building their own solutions, creating new technologies, and reimagining what their communities could look like.

The movement had started to grow, spreading like wildfire across the globe. There were grassroots projects in India, sustainable agriculture startups in Africa, and innovative energy solutions popping up in remote corners of South America. It was everything Lyana and her team had hoped for.

And yet, despite the progress, there was still a gnawing feeling in the pit of her stomach. A lingering doubt that wouldn't go away.

She heard the door to the roof open behind her and glanced back to see Max stepping out, his ever-present scowl in place, though it had softened in recent weeks.

"Thought I'd find you up here," he said, taking a seat next to her. "You're doing that brooding thing again."

Lyana smiled, shaking her head. "I don't brood. I reflect. Big difference."

Max smirked, looking out over the city with her. "So, what's on your mind? This whole thing actually seems to be working. People are waking up. It's what we wanted, right?"

Lyana nodded, though her expression remained pensive. "It is. But we both know this is just the beginning. They've woken up, but staying awake? That's the hard part. Humans have this way of falling back into old habits."

Max sighed, leaning back on his hands. "You're not wrong. I've seen it happen before—revolutions that fizzle out, ideas that get co-opted by the same forces they were fighting against. It's always a fight to keep the momentum going."

Lyana turned to look at him, her icy white hair catching the last rays of the setting sun. "Do you think they can do it? Really do it?"

Max hesitated, clearly weighing his answer. "Honestly? I don't know. But we've given them the tools. Whether they use them or not... that's up to them."

They sat in silence for a moment, watching the world below. The tide was shifting, yes, but the fragility of it all was palpable. The powers that had controlled the system for so long weren't going to give up without a fight. And even with the new wave of

160

innovators and entrepreneurs, the future of the planet still hung in the balance.

A Fragile Precipice

Back inside the headquarters, the rest of the team was gathered in the conference room, planning their next steps. Kai was hovering over a set of blueprints for a new tech hub they were building in Brazil, while Zora paced the room, discussing strategy with a group of their partners.

Kai looked up as Lyana and Max walked in, flashing his usual grin. "Good news! We've got another batch of grassroots projects launching in Southeast Asia. Turns out people really like the idea of saving the planet if you make it sound like an adventure."

Lyana laughed. "Well, we are saving the world one step at a time. Might as well make it fun."

Zora gave her a small smile, though her eyes were still focused. "The movement's growing faster than we anticipated. We've got thousands of people signing up for our workshops, and the number of new startups we're seeing in the sustainable tech sector is skyrocketing. But..." She trailed off, her expression darkening slightly.

"But?" Max prompted, crossing his arms.

Zora sighed, tapping her fingers on the table. "But the opposition isn't letting up. The corporations and governments haven't stopped. They're shifting their tactics—more subtle, more insidious. They're co-opting some of the language we've been using, pretending to be part of the movement while undermining it from within."

Lyana nodded, her earlier concerns bubbling back to the surface. "I knew they'd try to adapt. We're up against more than just greed. This is about maintaining control over people's futures."

Kai, ever the optimist, chimed in. "Look, we knew this was going to be a fight. But we're not backing down. And neither are the people we've inspired. They're not going to fall for the same old tricks."

Lyana smiled at him, appreciating his energy. "You're right. And we've got to keep pushing forward, no matter what they throw at us."

The team spent the next few hours strategizing, refining their plans, and discussing how to stay one step ahead of the forces that wanted to keep the world from changing. But even as they worked, Lyana couldn't shake the feeling that something bigger was coming. Something they hadn't yet anticipated.

Lyana Reflects

Later that night, long after the others had left, Lyana found herself back on the rooftop, staring up at the stars. The sky was clear, and the constellations twinkled brightly above her—each one a reminder of where she had come from and why she had chosen this path.

She thought of Lyra, her home, once so beautiful and full of promise, destroyed by forces that had spiraled out of control. She had seen what happened when a world lost its way, when people stopped dreaming, stopped innovating, and let corruption take hold.

Now, here on Earth, she was watching humanity teeter on that same edge.

For centuries, she had fought to give them a chance—to help them unlock their potential, to see that they could be so much more than they were. And now, finally, they were starting to believe it. But the question lingered: could they sustain it?

Could humans truly break free of the cycles that had held them down for so long? Could they push past the greed, the corruption, the fear, and build a future that was better, brighter?

Lyana sighed, running a hand through her hair as she gazed up at the stars. She wanted to believe they could. But she knew the fight wasn't over. Not by a long shot.

A voice interrupted her thoughts, pulling her back to reality. It was Max, standing in the doorway, watching her.

"You're thinking too much again," he said, his tone softer than usual.

Lyana smiled, nodding. "It's a habit. But can you blame me? We're on the brink of something huge. It feels... fragile."

Max walked over, standing beside her, and following her gaze to the sky. "Everything worth fighting for is fragile. But we've got something they don't."

"What's that?" she asked, turning to face him.

Max smirked. "Hope. And a whole lot of stubbornness."

Lyana laughed, shaking her head. "I guess that's true."

As the two of them stood there, staring out into the night, Lyana felt a flicker of something—hope, yes, but also a sense of determination. This wasn't the end of their journey. It was just the beginning.

A Cliffhanger of Possibility

The following day, Lyana gathered the Starseeds for one final meeting. They had accomplished so much, but there was still so much more to do. The world was waking up, but it was still fragile, still on the edge.

"Whatever comes next," she said, addressing her team, "we face it together. We've started something bigger than any of us, and we're not done yet. This is only the beginning."

The team nodded, their expressions a mix of resolve and excitement. They knew the challenges ahead, but they were ready for them.

As they left the meeting room, Lyana's phone buzzed. She glanced down at the screen and froze. It was a message—from someone she hadn't heard from in years.

"We need to talk. There's something coming. Something big. And it's not just about Earth."

Lyana's heart skipped a beat. She looked out at the city, the world she had fought so hard to save, and realized that the battle for humanity's future wasn't just theirs anymore.

The stars were calling again.

Chapter 19: More Starseeds Needed

Lyana stood at the edge of the roof, staring up at the stars, her thoughts swirling with the message she had just received. It had come through her hidden communication device, the one she hadn't used in years. The signal was weak, distant, but unmistakable. It was a warning from Lyra, a call from the remnants of a world long destroyed—but still, somehow, watching.

"The work is not done. Earth's future hangs in the balance. More Starseeds must awaken, or all will be lost."

The words echoed in her mind, refusing to fade.

She took a deep breath, her eyes tracing the constellations. The night sky had always been a comfort, a reminder that she wasn't alone, that somewhere out there were others like her—other Starseeds who had survived the destruction of Lyra and found their way to Earth. But now, the sky seemed heavier, the stars more distant, as if they too knew the gravity of what was coming.

Behind her, the door to the roof creaked open, and Zora stepped out, her face as calm and composed as ever, though Lyana could sense the concern just beneath the surface.

"I got your message," Zora said, walking over to stand beside her. "Another signal from Lyra?"

Lyana nodded, her voice quiet. "It's a warning. They're telling us that what we've done isn't enough. Earth is still on the brink, and if we don't awaken more Starseeds, everything we've worked for could collapse."

Zora sighed, crossing her arms as she looked out over the city. "More Starseeds... Do you think there are still that many of us out there? After all these years?"

166

Lyana glanced at her, her expression thoughtful. "I think so. We've been scattered across this planet for centuries. Some have blended in so well they've forgotten who they are. Others have been hiding, waiting for the right moment. But if we're going to turn this around—truly turn it around—we need them. All of them."

Zora frowned, her mind already calculating the next steps. "So, we need to find them. The ones still in hiding, the ones who've forgotten. We need to awaken them."

Lyana nodded, though the enormity of the task weighed heavily on her. They had already done so much building a movement, inspiring humanity, fighting back against corporate greed and systemic corruption. But now, it seemed as though their real challenge was just beginning.

A Warning from Lyra

Later that night, Lyana gathered the team in their makeshift headquarters, the old barn that had become both their sanctuary and their war room. Max, Kai, and Zora were already there, deep in conversation, when Lyana walked in, her face more serious than usual.

She didn't waste time with pleasantries.

"We've received a message from Lyra," she said, sitting down at the table. "It's a warning. They're telling us that more Starseeds need to be awakened if we're going to succeed."

Max leaned forward; his brow furrowed. "More Starseeds? You mean there are still others out there? How do we find them?"

Lyana shook her head. "We don't know exactly who or where they are. Some have been living here for centuries, blending in. Others have fallen so deep into their human lives that they've forgotten their true nature. But they're here. They've been here, just like us."

Kai, the optimist, grinned. "Well, that sounds like an adventure. We'll track them down, wake them up, and get this party started."

Zora gave him a look, but there was no denying the truth in his words. "It's going to be difficult," she said, her voice steady. "Some of them won't want to be found. And if they've forgotten who they are, we're going to need to find a way to remind them."

Lyana leaned back in her chair, her gaze distant. "I've been thinking about that. There are places—sacred places—where our energy is stronger, where Starseeds are more likely to remember who they are. We'll need to travel. We'll need to go to the places where our memories are the most vivid, the most connected to Lyra."

Max crossed his arms, clearly skeptical. "And what about the opposition? The corporations, the governments—they're not going to sit back and let us awaken more Starseeds without a fight."

"They won't," Lyana agreed. "But we're not just a handful of rebels anymore. We've got people on our side now. We've started a movement. And if we can gather more Starseeds, we'll have the strength we need to face whatever comes next."

Kai leaned forward; his eyes gleaming with excitement. "So, what's the plan? Where do we start?"

The Beginning of a New Quest

Lyana stood up, pacing as she spoke. "There are certain places on Earth where our energy—the energy of the

Starseeds—is stronger. Places where the veil between this world and the stars is thin. Stonehenge, the Pyramids of Giza, the Mayan ruins in Mexico... these places are not just historical sites. They're gateways. We need to go there and see if we can awaken the others."

Zora nodded, already mapping out the logistics in her mind. "We'll need to split up. There's too much ground to cover for us to stay together."

"Agreed," Max said. "But we need to be careful. If the corporations or governments catch wind of what we're doing, they'll try to stop us. They know we're the only ones standing in the way of their control."

Kai grinned, clearly relishing the challenge. "Let them try. We've outsmarted them before. Besides, this is the fun part— tracking down ancient Starseeds, unlocking hidden powers. It's like something out of a sci-fi movie."

Lyana smiled, despite the gravity of the situation. Kai's enthusiasm was contagious, and she was grateful for it. They were embarking on a journey that would test them in ways they hadn't anticipated, but they were ready.

"We leave tomorrow," she said, her voice firm. "I'll head to Egypt. Zora, you go to Stonehenge. Max, take South America— there are some places in the Andes that might hold the key. And Kai—well, you're going to need to be everywhere, aren't you?"

Kai laughed, already standing, and stretching. "You know me. I'm a man of many talents. I'll bounce around and cause some chaos where it's needed."

Zora rolled her eyes, but there was a small smile on her face. "Just don't blow anything up, Kai. At least not until we know what we're dealing with."

Lyana's Reflection

That night, as the others made their preparations, Lyana found herself back on the rooftop, staring up at the stars. She had always felt most connected to her home when she was under the open sky, the distant glow of the stars reminding her that she was more than just a woman running a tech company. She was a Starseed, part of something far greater than the small world of Earth.

But now, more than ever, she felt the weight of that responsibility. It wasn't just about guiding humanity anymore. It was about awakening the others—about gathering all the Starseeds who had been scattered across the globe and forgotten their true purpose.

This is just the beginning, she thought, her heart heavy but determined. The message from Lyra was clear: if Earth was to be saved, more Starseeds would have to rise. They couldn't do it alone. They would need every last one of them to push humanity forward, to break through the barriers of corruption and greed that still held so much power.

Lyana took a deep breath, her eyes still fixed on the stars. *I'm ready,* she told herself. *We're all ready.*

Tomorrow, they would begin the next phase of their mission. And this time, there was no turning back.

Chapter 20: The Mission Continues

Lyana stood in the center of the conference room, her fingers drumming against the sleek surface of the table as her team gathered around her. The air was electric with anticipation, though tinged with uncertainty. The next phase of their mission was about to begin, and while they had already overcome so much, the road ahead was anything but clear.

Max, Zora, and Kai sat on one side of the table, each wearing their unique expressions: Max with his usual grim determination, Zora deep in thought, and Kai... well, Kai was spinning in his chair, a wide grin plastered on his face as if they were planning a vacation rather than the next step in saving the planet.

"You know," Kai said, finally breaking the silence, "I've always wanted to visit Stonehenge. Do we get free passes to all the tourist sites when we do this whole 'awakening more Starseeds' thing, or is that an extra perk for saving the world?"

Zora rolled her eyes, but Lyana couldn't help but laugh. "If there's a discount for world-saving heroes, I'm sure you'll be the first to find it."

Kai spun again, grinning. "I'll settle for avoiding a global catastrophe. But hey, if there's time for a selfie with an ancient alien site, I'm game."

Max, who had been silent until now, leaned forward, cutting through the banter. "Joking aside, we need to focus. We're not just dealing with forgotten Starseeds. We're dealing with enemies who will stop at nothing to maintain their control. And if Lyra's message is anything to go by, this is bigger than any of us thought."

Lyana nodded; her expression serious once more. "Max is right. The forces that sabotaged us before haven't gone away.

172

They've only regrouped, and they'll be even more dangerous now that they know what we're capable of. That's why we need to be careful."

Zora crossed her arms, her tone thoughtful. "So, we split up, find the sacred sites, and wake the others. But how do we know they'll want to join us? Some Starseeds might have been in hiding for so long they've forgotten who they are—or worse, they might not want to be found."

"That's a risk we'll have to take," Lyana said, standing up and moving toward the center of the room. "But if we don't at least try, Earth doesn't stand a chance. We've already started something big, and we can't turn back now."

Preparing for the Journey

Over the next few days, the team prepared for their separate missions, each one tasked with visiting a different sacred site across the globe. The energy in the air was different now—more urgent, more charged with a sense of destiny. The Starseeds were no longer just fighting for innovation, entrepreneurship, or sustainability. They were fighting for Earth's survival, and the only way to win that fight was by awakening the others like them.

Lyana spent hours reviewing the maps, consulting ancient texts, and fine-tuning their plan. Kai, of course, had found a way to make the whole operation more entertaining. "Just in case we get bored," he said, handing Lyana a small device. "Think of it as a teleportation beacon. Or, if we're being honest, a really fancy way to bail out if things get too intense."

Lyana raised an eyebrow. "Teleportation? Since when did you become a sci-fi writer?"

Kai smirked. "Since I figured we might need a quick escape. Just don't tell Max. He'll start asking for safety protocols."

Lyana laughed, pocketing the device. "I won't. But let's try not to need it, okay?"

The preparations continued; each team member focused on their task. Max quietly worked on ensuring their resources were in place, Zora calculated every potential risk, and Kai—well, Kai somehow managed to keep everyone's spirits high, even as they prepared for what was likely to be the most dangerous mission they'd ever undertaken.

Sending the Signal

On the night before they were set to depart, Lyana found herself standing alone in the communications room, staring at the small console that had once been silent for so many years. Now, it was alive again, buzzing faintly with the possibility of connection.

She knew what she had to do. If they were going to succeed, they needed more than just their small group. They needed the others—the Starseeds who had gone into hiding, the ones who had blended so deeply into human life that they had forgotten their origins. Lyra's warning had been clear: if they didn't awaken more Starseeds, Earth's future would remain on a knife's edge.

Taking a deep breath, Lyana activated the console, sending out a signal—a call to every Starseed on Earth, wherever they might be.

The message was simple, yet powerful. It wasn't just a plea for help. It was a reminder of who they were, where they had come from, and what they were capable of.

"This is Lyana. If you're hearing this, you're one of us. The time has come to remember who you are. The time to hide is over. We need you. Earth needs you. Join us."

As the signal pulsed out into the night, spreading across the globe, Lyana felt a familiar sense of hope rise within her. The next stage of their journey had begun. Whether the others answered the call or not, only time would tell.

But for now, she had done all she could. It was up to the Starseeds to awaken.

A Cliffhanger: What Lies Ahead

The following morning, the team gathered one last time before setting off in different directions. Lyana stood at the head of the room, her gaze sweeping over each of them—Max, stoic but strong; Zora, focused and brilliant; and Kai, his mischievous grin never far from his lips.

"We've come a long way," Lyana said, her voice filled with both pride and determination. "But this is just the beginning. Whatever happens next, we face it together."

Max nodded, his usual gruffness softening slightly. "We'll be ready."

Zora adjusted her jacket, ever practical. "The plan is solid. We've accounted for every variable. Well, almost every variable."

"And if we run into trouble," Kai chimed in, flashing his teleportation beacon, "we've got a few tricks up our sleeves."

Lyana smiled, a mixture of excitement and apprehension filling her chest. The signal had been sent. The sacred sites were waiting. And somewhere, out there, more Starseeds were listening.

As they turned to leave, Lyana's phone buzzed in her pocket. She glanced at the screen and froze. It was a new message—encrypted, anonymous.

"I heard your call. We're coming. But so are they."

Her heart skipped a beat. The message was clear—there were others out there, both allies and enemies. The battle for Earth wasn't over. In fact, it was only just beginning.

"Let's move," she said, her voice steady as she pocketed the phone. "We've got work to do."

And with that, the Starseeds set off into the unknown, ready for whatever challenges awaited them.

The journey wasn't over. Not by a long shot.

To Be Continued...

Lyran Legacy: The Starseed Chronicles Begin

About the Author: Audrey Bell-Kearney

 Audrey Bell-Kearney is an entrepreneur, author, and visionary who recently discovered that she may be a Starseed from the star system Lyra. While she isn't entirely sure if this is true, the description of the Lyrans resonated with her in profound ways, inspiring her to create *The Lyran Legacy* as the first book in her eight-part series, *The Starseed Chronicles* under the imprint Starseed Media Group.

Audrey has written seven non-fiction books, mostly focused on entrepreneurship and business, but this venture into fiction is a new and exciting chapter for her. Though her first book was a collaboration between friends rather than a novel, she's never written fiction on this scale before. However, with the rise of smart writing tools, Audrey felt empowered to bring her big ideas and visionary storytelling to life.

"I've always wanted to be creative," Audrey says, "but my mind works in big ideas, business solutions, and strategies—not in weaving storylines. Smart writing tools have opened the door for me to explore new creative worlds, and I'm excited to complete the rest of the books in this series."

Audrey deeply admires those who can sit down and craft incredible works of fiction, acknowledging that the process comes naturally to some. For her, these new tools have provided a chance to escape into other realms and participate in a community she previously wasn't a part of—and she couldn't be more thrilled for the journey ahead.

When Audrey isn't writing or exploring her Starseed connection, she's the dynamic force behind the Gwinnett

Women's Chamber of Commerce, where she dedicates her time to helping small businesses grow. She's always creating content—whether it's for her business or for her new series—and looks forward to sharing these new adventures with her readers.

With *The Lyran Legacy*, Audrey Bell-Kearney invites you to join her on a cosmic journey, and she's just getting started.

Subscribe to the newsletter: www.TheBookPreneur.com

www.ingramcontent.com/pod-product-compliance
Lightning Source LLC
Chambersburg PA
CBHW031927280626
47169CB00019BA/2331